THE DEMON LOVER

'Veronica began to undress, and then she paused –
supposing what he had said were true – supposing
she were bound by an invisible chain which would
tighten and strangle her if she disobeyed Lucas –
why, then, she was in his hands, body and soul.
She could not run away, she could not cry out, and
yet her bonds would be invisible, imperceptible to
anyone but herself, and no one would believe her if
she told them; and even if she tried to tell them,
Lucas's power would descend upon her, choking,
strangling her, and she would be fighting for the air
that she was powerless to draw into her lungs. She
sat up in bed and with difficulty restrained herself
from shrieking aloud at the horror of her invisible
prison. She was indeed in a cage, a cage whose bars
were invisible. She could not claim the help or sympathy of her fellow beings; . . . The problem was
beyond her solution. Despairingly she settled down
upon the pillows to wait for dawn.'

DION FORTUNE

Perhaps no other occultist in the twentieth century has so fully combined a practical knowledge of magic with a thorough understanding of psychology as Dion Fortune. The first mass-market paperback editions of her famous novels are well overdue, marking as they do a peak of literary entertainment and a disturbingly authoritative introduction to the ancient teachings of the occult.

The series includes:

THE DEMON LOVER
MOON MAGIC
THE GOAT-FOOT GOD
THE WINGED BULL
THE SEA PRIESTESS

THE DEMON LOVER

Dion Fortune

A STAR BOOK
published by
WYNDHAM PUBLICATIONS

A Star Book
Published in 1976
by Wyndham Publications Ltd.
A Howard & Wyndham Company
123 King Street, London W6 9JG

First published in Great Britain by
The Aquarian Publishing Co. Ltd.

Printed in Great Britain by
Richard Clay (The Chaucer Press), Ltd., Bungay, Suffolk

ISBN 0 352 39892 2

CHAPTER ONE

At the back of one of the massive, old-fashioned houses in Bloomsbury Square was a single-storeyed structure originally intended by the architect for a billiard room. It was connected with the main building by a short passage, and its windowless walls supported a domed roof of glass. The present users of the room, however, were apparently engaged in some matter which did not require a good top light, for a ceiling had been built across the span of the dome, and save for the steady purring of an electric fan behind the louvre boards of the lantern, no sign of life was apparent from the outside, the windowless walls and double roofing rendering the building light and sound-proof. This suited admirably the purposes of its present users, whose work required absolute immunity from any sudden sound or change of light, and who had no wish to draw the attention of the neighbours to their proceedings.

Although the night was a sultry one, the group of men seated round the table seemed to suffer no inconvenience. The faces varied greatly in type; the chairman of the meeting had the air of a prosperous business man; on his right was an unmistakable lawyer; on his left, a benign old gentleman with a long white beard; opposite was a journalist. At the foot of the table, however, there sat a man who could not so readily be assigned to a place; he might have been a diplomat, he might have been a detective, or he might have been one of those pseudo-aristocratic adventurers who hang upon the fringe of smart society. He was the youngest man present, and the minute book in front of him marked him as the secretary of the meeting.

Though the members were of such divergent types, they had certain characteristics which marked them as men whom some common discipline had welded together. Each possessed the power of sitting absolutely motionless unless he had occasion to move, a far from common accomplishment; each radiated a peculiar sense of poise and power; and each, with the exception of the secretary, had a pair of absolutely expressionless eyes; and even his did not respond to emotion as eyes generally do, by alteration of the muscles round the sockets, but marked his feelings by an expansion and contraction of the pupil itself, which produced an extraordinary effect upon the observer. The eyes, of a very dark hazel with greenish lights in them, together with the sallowness of the skin, gave an unpleasing impression which, in some way, the perfect regularity of the features intensified. It was the face of a man who might be exceedingly interesting, exceedingly charming, and exceedingly unscrupulous.

The meeting, proceeding quietly with the transaction of business, was redeemed from ordinariness by the fact that the seventh member lay asleep on a couch, no one taking the slightest notice of him except the secretary, who cast quick, sidelong glances in his direction in the intervals of note-taking, and seemed prepared to spring up and catch him should he show any signs of rolling on to the floor.

The discussion of business was carried on quietly, almost in undertones; accounts for large sums of money being brought forward and passed without comment, when a peculiar sound broke the stillness of the room; from the figure on the couch came a long-drawn-out sibilant hiss. No notice of this strange manifestation was taken by any person present except the secretary, who put a cross on the top of the pad on which he was taking notes. A short while passed, during which the committee still worked in hushed voices, and then a second prolonged hiss came from the

6

sleeper, and the secretary made a second cross on his writing pad. A third and fourth hiss followed in quick succession, and successive crosses were added to the row at the top of the secretary's tablet. On the completion of the fourth he looked up as if anticipating a command. For the first time the other members of the committee glanced at the sleeping figure.

'If he is sufficiently deep in trance,' said the chairman, 'we will put aside the accounts and proceed with the Housmann problem.'

'He is on the fourth hypnoidal level,' said the secretary.

'That will do,' was the answer, and with cautious movements the committee disposed itself so that the hitherto ignored seventh member became the focus of attention.

The secretary stretched out a thin brown hand and tilted the shade of the lamp so that the sleeper's face was thrown into still deeper shadow, then he left his chair and went and sat on the couch beside the recumbent man, who never stirred; leaning forward, he tapped a certain spot on the unconscious head with a peculiar rhythm. Immediately, without stirring a muscle of his face, the sleeper emitted the most extraordinary sound that ever issued from a human throat – it could only be compared to the weird noises that arise from a faulty transmitter/receiver – and then the secretary proceeded in as calm and matter of fact manner as if he were using an ordinary telephone, to ask for a number, using the unconscious man as a means of communication.

'Fifty North, fourteen East,' he repeated several times, as if seeking to call up some invisible exchange. After a few repetitions the sleeping man replied in the German language, asking his interrogator who was calling.

'Thirty, nought,' replied the secretary. 'Is that the Prague Lodge?'

'It is,' replied the sleeper, speaking in English, with a slight foreign accent.

'We want particulars of Brother Hermann Housmann, a

German American, last heard of at Prague, who is suspected of attempting to negotiate with the Vatican for the sale of information concerning the Brotherhood's policy in regard to the French situation.'

'He left here early in May for Switzerland. Try the Geneva Lodge,' replied the sleeper.

Again the secretary repeated his tapping, and again the peculiar note, half-way between the hoot of an owl and a telephone bell, was heard.

'Forty-six North, six East,' said the secretary, and the sleeping man replied in French this time, asking again who called.

'Thirty, nought,' replied the secretary again, and again inquired of the sleeper for news of Hermann Housmann, and was informed that he had left Geneva at the end of May and proceeded to Naples and thence to New York.

Yet once more the secretary repeated his tapping, and elicited the same peculiar sound from the sleeper.

'Forty, North, seventy-four West,' he repeated several times, and finally a voice with a strong American accent replied. News of Hermann Housmann was again demanded, and this time obtained.

'He came here early in June and got in touch with the Tammany bosses. We sent him a summons to attend Lodge, and he got in a panic and started West. Then it was decided to send him an order of execution by means of the Dark Ray of Destruction.'

The men round the table stirred uneasily and looked at one another.

'With what results?' asked the interrogator.

'He stopped off at Buffalo, took the cars to Niagara, and went over the suspension bridge.'

'Over into Canada?'

'No, over into the river,' replied the sleeper, his expressionless countenance strangely contradicted by the challenging note in his voice.

The men in the dimly-lit room looked at each other. The

8

journalist shrugged his shoulders; the lawyer fidgeted with pens and paper, and the pupils of the secretary's eyes opened and shut like those of a cat. It was the patriarch on the chairman's left who broke the silence.

'I don't like it,' he said. 'I don't like it at all. I cannot approve of these methods. For God's sake let us leave the issue to higher intelligences than ours, and not take the law into our own hands.'

'There is a spirit growing up in the Fraternity,' said the chairman, in a deep, booming voice, 'which can lead to nothing but disaster,' and he glared at the secretary as if he were responsible for the American's death. The pupils of the secretary's peculiar eyes completely disappeared, and the irises filled with green gleams like the fire in a black opal, but it was the journalist who took up the defence.

'This is no time for half measures,' he said. 'Be sure your policy is right, and then go ahead and make a clean job of it. Look at the difference in our position since the new spirit came into the Fraternity, from being a group of anti-quarians, we have become a factor to be reckoned with in international politics.'

One after another they spoke with considerable feeling, but the secretary kept silence; he, although he was never directly addressed, seemed to be regarded by the others as responsible for the new spirit. Finally, each having said his say, silence fell upon the men round the table. The secretary raised his peculiar eyes to the chairman.

'Shall I bring him round?' he inquired.

The chairman nodded glumly. The brown hand of the secretary passed swiftly across the face of the sleeper with a peculiar snatching movement several times repeated, who thereupon stirred slightly and snuggled down into the cushions. It was apparent, however, that the death-like passivity had given place to natural sleep. In a minute or two he stirred again, roused, sat up, and blinked dazedly at the lamp. The secretary poured a cup of steaming coffee from a vacuum flask and handed it to him, for close though

9

the night was, the man was shivering with cold. The hot drink speedily restored him to his normal consciousness, and he inquired whether any news had been obtained of Hermann Housmann, and the words that had issued from his lips were repeated to him. At the news of the suicide he gave a long whistle and stared hard at the secretary.

Presently the meeting broke up, the members departing in twos and threes; at the door each of these sober-minded men of the world did a peculiar thing, they turned and genuflected as if leaving a church, for in the shadows in the far end of the room the dim outline of an altar could be discerned on which a red light was burning.

Among the last to leave was the old man with the long white beard. Pausing before the secretary, he held out his corded old hand. After an almost imperceptible hesitation, the thin brown fingers were placed in it.

'Lucas,' said the old man, 'no one appreciates more than I do what your work has meant to the Fraternity, but I hope to God you will never want anything you ought not to have.'

Left alone, the secretary switched off the electric fan and silence shut down upon the room like a thing palpable. He paused for a moment with his hand on the switch, as if uncertain what to do next, then he crossed over to the table and stood looking down at the scattered papers, but made no movement to gather them up; he was evidently deep in thought, going over in his mind the events of the evening and trying to interpret their significance. It had been quite evident that he was not in good odour; even his supporters had been apologists and his opponents had been among the weightiest members of the Fraternity, and the evening's proceedings had served to bring to the surface a dissatisfaction that had been smouldering for some time. Lucas's doings were not liked, so much had been made quite clear to him; and if his doings were not liked, then he must be

10

prepared to mend his ways or there would be serious trouble, for it is one thing to get into an occult fraternity, but quite another to get out of it.

He knew his chiefs, men of the highest ideals, but also of the sternest justice, and he knew that rebellion need expect no mercy. First would come an order to attend Lodge and offer an explanation; should that prove unsatisfactory, he would be commanded to return to the archives all insignia, symbols, and manuscripts, and he would be solemnly warned, in a formula thousands of years old, that for the future he would exercise occult powers at his peril; and then he would be bidden to go forth and associate no more with his brethren.

Should he, however, persist in his evil ways, should he, especially, pervert to his own ends the powers he had acquired, then something that was not of this plane of existence dealt with him. No man raised a finger against him, the law was not invoked, his name was not mentioned for evil, but, all the same, something happened to him, and after that he was incapable of either good or evil for the short span of existence which usually remained to him.

Lucas knew all this quite well, and, hands deep in trouser pockets, he slowly paced the room, calculating his chances of escape should he decide on the course of defiance.

Six years ago, with a promising journalistic career before him, he had suddenly abandoned Fleet Street, and to the surprise and disgust of his colleagues, become secretary to a society for the study of comparative folk-lore. Why he did it, they could not make out, and Lucas did not enlighten them; but, if the truth were known, he was controlling the mundane *pied-à-terre* that even the most esoteric of occult fraternities must have, and to this fraternity he dedicated his existence. As had been truly said that evening, he had raised the Fraternity to a very different position to that which it had occupied when first he took its affairs in hand. He had found it engaged in study for study's sake, and he had shown it the practical application of its knowledge.

11

Hitherto it had contented itself in dealing with the individual, his development or regeneration. Lucas showed it that its methods were equally applicable to international affairs, and he had interfered with such notable success in certain *coups d'état* that the great majority of his Fraternity looked upon him as the coming leader. It was only a minority that viewed his doings askance, but, as he had seen that evening, the seniors of the Fraternity were in that minority to a man, and it was they alone who could bind or loose. It was useless to have the support of numbers if those who held the keys of power closed the door upon him, and it had been borne in upon Lucas recently that these doors were closed, had, in fact, been closed for some time. He had realized that no amount of hard work, no amount of devotion, would take a man up the Fraternity if that man's heart were not right. Lip service would not avail, either; the trained clairvoyants who had charge of these matters judged a man neither by what he said nor what he did, but by the colours of his aura, and that tell-tale emanation revealed the truth. No amount of ostentatious church-going on Sundays and wearing of crosses on watch-chains could conceal the dull red glow that Saturday night's diversions left behind, or counterfeit the bright clear electric blue that had to show before a man was judged fit for the higher degrees.

Lucas knew that although his aura showed the occult green, that green was not right, and he could not get it right except by changing his whole nature, by casting out the inordinate ambition and love of power that consumed him and bringing in compassion for his fellow men, and neither of these things could Lucas see his way to achieve; he despised his fellow man too much to feel anything beyond a contemptuous pity for him; and as for foregoing the fruits of power, what else was there to live and strive for? He was quite willing to show kindness to all and sundry, or any other manifestation in fact that might be demanded of him as a qualification, but laboriously to acquire power and

12

then to refrain from using it for one's own benefit even when driven into a corner, this was beyond his comprehension. He was prepared to pay any price required for his apprenticeship, he had worked as Jacob worked for Rachel, but for two years his progress had been held up, and men with half his capacities had preceded him into the higher degrees. His theoretical studies completed, he realized that the chiefs had no intention of entrusting him with the practical applications thereof. The secret science of the hidden forces of man and nature he knew, but not the Names of Power by which these forces were controlled, and without them all his studies were useless – he had the lock, but not the key.

And so he paced up and down, pondering his problem. The chiefs had openly declared their dissatisfaction; a complete revision of the Fraternity's policy might follow, and with it a drastic clipping of his own wings; he might even be removed from the post of secretary. For this contingency he had endeavoured to provide. Next door lived an aged general, gasping his life out in repeated attacks of bronchitis, any one of which might prove fatal; Lucas had judiciously cultivated his acquaintance, and the first use he had made of his Delta Degree initiation was to use the powers it conferred to cause the old man to make a will in his favour, so Lucas hoped before long to find himself among the landed gentry and the possessor of private means, in which situation he thought it might be easier for him to come up to the moral standard of the Fraternity and obtain the coveted higher degrees. His only danger was that the will might be contested and the transaction thus brought to the ears of his chiefs, and what they would have to say on the subject would not be pleasant hearing, for he knew full well the white occultist's horror of black magic, and his drastic methods of dealing with it, and he supposed they would consider his transactions very black indeed, though he had no intention whatever of doing harm with the money, which would, he thought, be used to much better advantage if it were in his hands than distributed among the general's nephews and nieces of the third and fourth generation.

All the same, Lucas had a very wholesome fear of the dark force which almost invariably got the man, sooner or later, who deviated from the right-hand path. Some, indeed, but not many, had had immunity; but they were men who had climbed so high before they turned to the left that they were senior to those who had to deal with them and often, in fact, returned the occult onslaughts in kind; but these favoured individuals were rare; few men maintained themselves long when the Fraternity moved against them.

So Lucas calculated his prospects, and they did not look to him very promising unless he could get hold of those Words of Power that should enable him to fight at least on a level footing. That evening had shown him clearly that the Fraternity would not give them to him; how, in the name of Heaven, earth, and the waters under the earth could those carefully guarded secrets be obtained? Lucas's stride lengthened and quickened as his perplexity increased. Gazing before him with unseeing eyes, he swung like a pendulum up and down the room.

Suddenly his progress was arrested. His blind march had gradually edged him across the floor till he ran into the low couch upon which the man who had served as the receiver of the occult telephone had lain. He stood staring down at it as if the sleeper still lay there, and through those entranced lips might come the solution of his problem. And come it did. With a sudden start Lucas realized that anyone who could go into a sufficiently deep trance could 'listen in' at the occult ceremonies and learn the Words of Power – provided he cared to take the risk! Lucas had nerves of steel as an occultist needs to have, but even he did not care about that risk.

Still he stood looking down at that couch, seeking further inspiration from a source that had already proved so fruitful. Supposing he could 'get at' Spencer, and get him to

14

join him in this raid upon the secrets of the Fraternity? But he dismissed the idea; the brethren were all picked men, hard to corrupt by either threats or promises; besides, Spencer wouldn't like the risk any more than he did, but the idea in itself was good. Supposing he could find a trance medium who did not know enough to be scared, he could have his own occult telephone and 'listen in' with impunity. The powers might 'strafe' the medium, but they would find it exceedingly difficult to locate the man who was operating the medium.

Lucas thoughtfully gathered up the papers, put the lights out, and went to bed.

CHAPTER TWO

When a school breaks up for the summer holidays it is usual for the pupils to go their various ways to their various homes. All are not so happily placed, however, and the pupil who stepped out of the dark entry of the business training college into the blazing sunshine was engaged upon the urgent quest of fresh work now that her secretarial course was finished. Only the most rigorous self-denial had enabled her to get through her training; the third term had been one of semi-starvation, and this, added to the strain of the final examinations, had reduced her to an abnormal state in which she floated rather than walked, and saw grey ghosts about her instead of men and women.

In her hand she grasped an envelope bearing an address in a neighbouring square, and containing an account of her attainments and credentials, and in her heart was a gnawing anxiety as to what she should do if she failed to obtain the prospective post. Three other girls joined her on the sunlit pavement, also bearing envelopes, and demanded of her her destination, which proved to be the same as her own, and her heart sank still further when she realized that there was going to be competition for the coveted work, and into her mind there flashed a vision of her own face as she had seen it in the dressing-room glass while pinning on her hat – white and exhausted, with deep lines under the eyes and dark circles round them, and it seemed to her that, were she herself engaging a secretary, Veronica Mainwaring would not be her choice.

The others chattered gaily on their way to the square, they did not care much whether they got the post or not, they were only looking at it in case it were so well worth taking as to counterbalance the loss of a summer holiday, and they made it quite plain to Veronica that it had to be *very* good to be accepted by them at that time of year. She, for her part, had determined to accept anyone who would have her, rather than be disengaged in the blank emptiness of a London summer.

They were admitted through large double doors by an impassive butler, and ushered into a room which was obviously a waiting-room rather than one that was lived in. Veronica, in her abnormal, almost dream state, felt as if the spirit of the place was audible to her inner consciousness; the butler did not seem to her to be an ordinary butler, but rather a lay brother of some sort of fraternity; she wondered whether the immaculate shirt-front concealed a great cross that hung from his neck by a chain, or was it the symbol of some strange pagan worship he wore? She felt certain that the carefully arranged strands of hair disposed at regular intervals across the top of his bald head rested upon a store of knowledge such as is not usually confined under a butler's skull. The atmosphere of the room, while full of strange, almost electrical vibrations, was brooded over by a great peace, wonderfully soothing to the girl's overwrought nerves. A longing to remain in the stillness overwhelmed her, but she feared greatly less the coveted post were not for her, for half the secretarial agencies of London appeared to have sent candidates of all shapes, sizes, and descriptions.

Suddenly the door opened and a man stood on the threshold surveying the assembly. Of medium height and lightly built, he moved with a springy alertness that put Veronica in mind of a stag, as if he could be off and away at full speed in the flash of a second. Deliberately and entirely impersonally, he inspected the waiting women one by one. Finally Veronica's turn came for a scrutiny. The man's

17

eyes met hers with a normal, observant, not unsympathetic glance, and then, all of a sudden, changed to an expression of ferocious intensity, and yet he did not appear to see her at all, but, on the contrary, to be looking straight through her. A second later he resumed his normal expression, and for the first time since entering the room, he spoke.

'If you will come to my office,' he said, 'I should like to have a talk with you.'

Veronica followed him out of the room into the one immediately behind it. It was a large, pleasant room, furnished not as an office, but as a sitting-room, and surrounded by book-cases. A faint, sweet smell, as if incense were habitually burnt there, hung in the air. The door of a strong room, and a desk in the window, were the sole indications that it was used for business purposes.

The man seated himself at the desk and motioned her to a chair opposite.

'My name is Lucas,' he said, 'what is yours?'

She told him, and with shaking fingers handed him her training certificate, which he accepted, but neglected to remove from its envelope.

'How old are you?' was the next question.

'Twenty-three,' said Veronica.

'What did you do previous to your training?'

She told him how she had cared for her widowed mother till the latter's death terminated the little pension upon which they had both subsisted, and then how the minute savings had just served to launch her upon the world.

'Have you good health?' he inquired. 'In the ordinary way, that is, when you are not overworked? Have you had any serious illnesses?'

She was able to give satisfactory answers to both these questions.

'I think you will do,' said the man. 'What salary do you want?'

Veronica had had so little hope of obtaining the post that she had not thought about the salary, and almost at ran-

18

dom, stated the sum that one of her companions had remarked would be necessary to secure her own services, and then her heart stood still lest she had demanded too much and would be rejected, but the man in the revolving chair did not seem disconcerted, he nodded his head.

'We will see how it works,' he said. 'Now when can you start?'

Veronica said that she was disengaged and could start forthwith.

'That will suit me very well,' he said. 'There is no occasion for delay; if we are going to begin, we may as well begin at once. You will have a couple of rooms upstairs placed at your disposal; I live in the house myself, but that need not trouble you, you will never see me except during business hours. Various other men come and go. I don't know whether you will consider the butler's wife an adequate chaperone, but she is the best we can offer you. Get a taxi and bring your things round right away.'

Veronica accepted. The offer was beyond her hopes. She asked no questions, she did not even permit her mind to question, she literally flung herself into this haven of refuge and thanked whatever gods might be. Lucas himself let her out of the front door and watched her for a moment as she walked down the road, a little smile curling his lips. He was evidently well pleased with his bargain.

Veronica returned to the hostel that had been her home during the long months she had worked at the training school. There was little enough in her cubicle to pack, and, having put her meagre belongings together, she went to the office to pay her bill.

'Where shall we send your letters?' asked the superintendent.

Veronica gave the address.

'So you have got a resident post. What work are you going to do?'

Not until the question was put to her did Veronica realize that she had never inquired the nature of the work

19

on which she was about to be engaged, any more than Lucas had inquired as to her capacities or references. Reluctantly she admitted her ignorance.

'But, Miss Mainwaring, you do not mean to say that you have accepted a post, and a resident post too, without inquiring who you were working for? Perhaps you don't even know whether it is a man or a woman?'

'It is a man,' said Veronica, 'and his name is Lucas,' and she realized that that was absolutely all she knew. She did not even know what would be her hours of duties, what demands he would make on her, or what qualifications she would require, and she suddenly remembered that he was paying her as a resident secretary the salary she had demanded believing she would have to support herself. Surely exceptional requirements must condition the payment of such a salary.

'I do not feel at all happy about you,' said the superintendent. 'But at any rate you are near here, so you must come round and let us know how you get on.'

Veronica wished her good-bye and transported her few belongings in a taxi round to the house in the square. The impassive butler again admitted her, and again Veronica experienced the sensation that she was in a church. The strange, indescribable feeling of remoteness and stillness enveloped her. A pleasant-faced woman appeared from the nether regions and conducted her to two rooms upon an upper floor. They looked straight into the heart of a great plane tree that stood in the garden of the next house, for the whole of the back premises of the house she was in were occupied by a large, one-storey annexe.

The rooms led one out of the other, pleasant, old-fashioned rooms with deep window-seats to the bow windows. Big sash windows let in the light, and heavy wooden shutters, folding back into the walls, were equally capable of shutting out both light and air. A capacious grate bore witness to the good old days of plenty, and, glimpsed through the open door of the adjoining room, a high feather bed with a curtained canopy declared that the tradition was not forgotten, and that the present owners of the house also knew what comfort, if not what hygiene, meant.

Her reverie was interrupted by the butler's voice. 'We will send up your dinner at seven, Miss. All your meals will be served up here.'

'Will Mr Lucas want me this evening?' she asked.

'I don't know, Miss, he is out at present'; and she was left to her own devices with instructions to ring for anything she required.

Her unpacking disposed of, she sat on the broad, repp-covered window-seat watching the birds in the tree. She had a curious feeling that she was a prisoner, free in appearance, as the lions on the Mappin terraces are free, yet ringed round upon every side by invisible barriers. She wished the superintendent had kept silence and refrained from instilling that uneasy doubt. Why could not people leave one to one's own devices? True, she did not know the nature of her work or the occupation of Lucas, but why should things be wrong?

The butler's wife came up with a tray, and Veronica determined to make good the deficiencies in her knowledge by judicious questioning.

'Have you been here long, Mrs Ashlott?'

'Lor – Yes, Miss. I come here when I married. Ashlott's been here, man and boy, these forty years.'

'Has Mr Lucas been here long?'

'No, Miss. Only five or six years. He is quite a new-comer.'

'Does anyone else live in the house beside Mr Lucas?'

'No, Miss. Only you and me and Ashlott but the gentle-men are always coming and going, and we often put them up for the night. I always keeps the beds made up.'

'What is Mr Lucas?' asked Veronica boldly.

'Secretary, Miss.'

'Oh!' said Veronica. 'And the gentlemen? What are they?'

'Ah,' said Mrs Ashlott. 'Now you're asking.' With which cryptic utterance she departed.

It was after ten o'clock, and Veronica was thinking of bed when there came a knock at the door, and in response to her summons, Lucas entered.

'Don't get up,' he said as she rose nervously, the superintendent's suspicions flashing through her mind. 'I won't keep you long. I only wanted to explain to you one or two things about your job. The work comes in rushes, and unexpectedly, at all hours of the twenty-four, in fact, so I don't want you to go out for the next few days, but to be in the house so that I can get you if I want you suddenly. After that, if I decide to keep you on, I will make arrangements for you to have regular time off duty. The work is not exacting, a good part of the time you will have nothing whatever to do, but I want you to be at hand in case I need you.'

Veronica's heart had sunk while he was speaking. So her post was not yet a security? The uncertainty, and the renewed anxiety it engendered, made her acquiesce very humbly to Lucas's request that she should not leave the house for the next few days. He remained for a few minutes, chatting with her pleasantly and kindly, evidently wishing to put her at her ease and make her feel settled and contented. Moreover, his words had done their work; Veronica, secure of her post, might have been tempted to question and criticize the conditions of it, but Veronica, insecure, clung desperately, dreading to find herself out of work. At all costs she must keep this, her first post, long enough to have a respectable reference. With a single phrase he had ensured her obedience. For one week she would accept the most eccentric commands without question, she would humour him to the top of his bent, refuse nothing, protest against nothing. And a week was all that Lucas required for the installing of his occult telephone.

*

The next morning Veronica awaited her employer's pleasure at nine; likewise at ten, but he did not come; finally at eleven he appeared, smelling pleasantly of soap and very spick and span and cheerful, and the morning's work commenced. Veronica found that hers was to be the appalling task of copying voluminous documents, every one of which was in cypher; letter by letter, the weird gibberish had to be copied and then counter-checked. When the copying was finished, however, there seemed to be nothing else for her to do; Lucas himself worked indefatigably, but apparently did not see fit to entrust her with any further tasks. She sat at her desk, hands folded, watching his bent back. Time went on, and time went on, and still he worked, and still she waited. At one o'clock he called a halt for lunch, bidding her return at two. But when she returned at that hour and inquired what she was to do next, he appeared somewhat nonplussed, as if he had not been expecting such an inquiry, and looked vaguely round at the furniture, as if it might be in need of her services. No response being forthcoming, his gaze returned to Veronica, and she fancied that he was trying not to smile.

'I have nothing for you to do at the moment,' he said. 'You can have a look at these if you like,' and he pointed to a pile of morning papers lying on a chair.

Veronica read the journalistic description of doom and disaster until five o'clock, when Lucas, who had worked unintermittently, rose, stretched himself, and announced that he had to go out.

'Will you want me again this evening?' asked Veronica.

He shook his head. 'I shall not come back till late.'

'Then would you mind if I just ran round to the hostel? It is only in the next square. The superintendent asked me to go in and see her.'

Veronica raised her eyes to his as she spoke, and saw to her amazement that the pupils had entirely disappeared; two greenish-brown discs looked back at her without a trace of expression, inhuman, malignant, horrible. Anything more sinister it would be impossible to imagine than this human countenance from which all trace of humanity had suddenly been erased. She stood rooted to the floor, gazing at this horror till Lucas's voice broke the spell.

'I would prefer you did not go out for the present, as I have already told you,' he said. 'Someone might ring up on the phone,' he added, by way of explanation. The pupils of his eyes were slowly returning to their normal proportions. He looked at her sharply, perceiving her consternation. 'What is the matter?' he asked.

'Nothing,' said Veronica. She could not very well explain to him that it was the horror of his face that had overcome her. He continued to stare at her, not with the offensive stare of a man's curiosity, but with an entirely impersonal inspection. Apparently the result was unsatisfactory, for he took a step towards her. Instinctively Veronica stepped back. Lucas took another step, and Veronica again retreated; she was against the desk now, and could go no further, and Lucas came right up to her and looked into her eyes; she was powerless to withdraw them and gazed back at him helpless, fascinated. He was not a tall man, and his face was almost on a level with hers, but a sense of power issued from him that held her spellbound. She looked and looked, and did not wish to turn away; vitality radiated from those eyes, intense, magnetic, compelling. Veronica went on looking.

She might have stood thus till she turned to stone if the man himself had not released her. Something shut down in his eyes, the power was cut off, and she was looking into an ordinary human countenance, olive-skinned, clear-cut, far from unprepossessing. Her horror of him was gone, in its place remained a curious fascination; what was he going to do next? She wanted to see. Her eyes followed every movement he made about the room. She knew that he was aware of this scrutiny, that he expected it, did not resent it. She was sorry now that he was going out; everything would seem very flat and lifeless when he was gone. He looked up,

24

caught her eyes, and smiled. She did not attempt to turn away.

'Go upstairs to your rooms,' he said. 'Mrs Ashlott will bring you your supper. You will do all right.'

Obediently she went towards the door, he opened it to let her out, and she went upstairs. As she turned at the half landing she saw that he was still looking after her, his eyes sparkling with some secret satisfaction. Dully she wondered what it might be, but her mind for the moment seemed at a standstill and refused its service. She went up to her room and flinging herself upon the bed, fell into a deep sleep from which she was only awakened by the appearance of Mrs Ashlott with her supper tray two hours later.

She did not feel hungry, but made some pretence of eating her supper, for the sake of Mrs Ashlott. Then, the meal dispatched, she sat on the window-seat, watching the setting sun. All her uneasiness was gone; she was placid, contented, non-thinking. She gazed at the great red globe, shorn of its power by the thick London atmosphere, with a face as expressionless as its own. Slowly it sank. Its rim touched the horizon. Gradually it disappeared. With its going a change occurred. The room felt suddenly cold, close August night though it was. Veronica sat up, and pulled herself together with a little shiver. What was it? What was the matter? Then with a rush the horror of Lucas's eyes returned to her. She sprang to her feet. What house was this that she was in? The Ashlotts, Lucas, the mysterious 'gentlemen'? Who and what were they all? And she – was she trapped? Did Lucas not intend to let her out? and if so, what did he mean to do with her? What was his motive? Was it all real or was it a nightmare? One thing was quite clear, she would not stop another second in this awful place, she must get out of it at all costs. Nothing mattered compared to that.

She put on her hat, and caught up her purse. Her things did not matter, she could send for those later. Down the passage she sped on tip-toe, her feet making no sound on the thick dark carpet. But in an alcove was a settee, and on the settee a man sat reading. It was Lucas.

'I thought you would,' he said, without looking up.

Veronica was desperate. For a moment she stood poised, checked in mid-career, then she sprang forward again. Lucas did not hear her, the heavy carpet gave back no sound, and she was a dozen feet down the passage before he noticed her manoeuvre. She literally hurled herself down the stairs, hardly touching the steps with her feet, swung herself round the bend by the banisters and was off down the next flight. There was a thud behind her as Lucas jumped the whole flight and landed in the passage. Then she felt herself caught from behind, and her elbows pinned to her sides. She screamed shrilly, and a hand was clapped over her mouth. Desperately she struggled till the arm that encircled her shifted its grip and clutched her into breathless immobility. Then they remained motionless.

It was the first time that Veronica had had closer contact with a man than the conventional handshake, and her first sensation was utter astonishment, his strength was so much greater than she had expected. He was so surprisingly hard too, as a sinewy forearm pinned her ruthlessly against his chest; and he smelt of strong pipe tobacco and shaving soap, strange, unfamiliar unfeminine smells. Veronica was so taken up with her observations that she forgot to be frightened till she felt Lucas shift his grip from her breast to her waist, and with the breath half crushed out of her, carry her downstairs and drop her unceremoniously among the cushions of the office sofa.

He stood back and inspected her, smoothing his ruffled hair, breathless, laughing. Veronica straightened her skirts and gathered together the shreds of her dignity.

'I wish to leave,' she said.

'Do you?' said Lucas, tucking the ends of his tie back into his waistcoat. 'I am afraid I can't spare you.'

'Why not?'

'You happen to be useful to me.'

26

'But you can get another secretary.'

'I don't want a secretary.'

'Then – then why did you engage me?'

'You would not understand if I told you, my dear child, so there is no use wasting time in explanations.'

He pulled down his waistcoat, shot forward his cuffs, and adjusted his coat collar; then, these preliminaries concluded, he gave Veronica his undivided attention. For several seconds they returned each other's gaze, then Lucas reached forward a thin brown forefinger and touched the soft round girlish throat.

'There is something round your neck,' he said.

Up went Veronica's hand involuntarily.

'Look,' he said, 'it is a steel collar.'

The image his words evoked flashed into her mind, and as it did so, she felt cold hard metal under her hand.

'There is a steel chain attached to it,' the man's soft level voice continued. 'A slender steel chain. Run your hand down it.'

He took her hand in his and drew it towards him, and she felt the links run through her fingers.

'And I hold the end of it,' he added significantly. 'If you try to call out, or to tell what I do not wish told, that collar will contract till it strangles you. Feel, it is contracting now.'

Veronica felt something rigid grip her about the throat. The pressure steadily increased. She gasped and fought for air as the trachea closed. Then Lucas touched her forehead.

'It has relaxed now,' he said, 'but remember, this will happen again if ever you try to give me away.'

Veronica drew in a great lungful of air and rose to her feet. She was too perplexed to feel frightened. Lucas was smiling at her pleasantly.

'Go to bed now,' he said. 'Sleep well, pleasant dreams. Ten o'clock tomorrow morning.'

CHAPTER THREE

Veronica went to her room, but sleep was another matter. What motive could Lucas possibly have in retaining a not very brilliant shorthand-typist against her will? He had not attempted to make love to her, his touch had been by no manner of means a caress, in fact he had handled her as if she had been a recalcitrant puppy. Veronica had a very distinct remembrance of that strangulating pressure on her throat; would that really occur if she tried to break away from Lucas? Would she feel that awful tightening – that inability to breathe – if she attempted to appeal to others for help? If so, then she were trapped indeed.

Utterly bewildered, she sat on her bed staring through the wide open window into the warm summer night. It was too late to try the experiment now, but she determined to arise at daybreak and slip out before the household were awake. Comforted by this thought Veronica began to undress, and then she paused – supposing what he had said were true – supposing she were bound by an invisible chain which would tighten and strangle her if she disobeyed Lucas – why, then, she was in his hands, body and soul. She could not run away, she could not cry out, and yet her bonds would be invisible, imperceptible to anyone but herself, and no one would believe her if she told them; and even if she tried to tell them, Lucas's power would descend upon her, choking, strangling her, and she would be fighting for the air that she was powerless to draw into her lungs. She sat up in bed and with difficulty restrained herself from shrieking aloud at the horror of her invisible prison.

She was indeed in a cage, a cage whose bars were invisible. She could not claim the help or sympathy of her fellow beings; she was as much alone as if Lucas had transferred her to another planet. She had a notion that Ashlott might understand, but she was quite sure he would not help; but the policeman at the corner, the superintendent of the hostel, if she appealed to them for help would think she was insane, and yet that collar and chain were quite real enough to strangle her. The problem was beyond her solution. Despairingly she settled down upon the pillows to wait for dawn.

Downstairs in the office Lucas was writing up his diary. A green-shaded lamp cast a circle of bright light on the desk and the rest of the room was in darkness. The events of the day had apparently been much to his liking, for a little smile curled his lips as he wrote.

'Things came to a head this afternoon,' the neat small writing, clear as print, advanced along the lines of the book in front of him. 'Had to put the cards on the table sooner than I expected, but found V.M. very suggestible and got her well in hand, and do not anticipate any difficulty in putting her into a trance. Think she ought to do very well provided her body will hold together, but her physique is frail and she has been badly over-strained. Have told Mrs Ashlott to feed her up well. Mrs A. thinks I have a kind heart. V.M. tried to bolt. Chased her down stairs and carried her into the office where I suggested to her that I had put a collar and chain on her. She took the suggestion very well. Told her that the collar would strangle her if she tried to talk, and she nearly choked; very curious, same mechanism as asthma. Shall have to be careful not to choke her altogether.'

Lucas locked the book and put it away in his private safe. Yes, he had every reason to be satisfied with the day's work. He had backed his clairvoyance to enable him to pick out a potential psychic from the miscellaneous collection of women the secretarial agencies had sent him and it looked as if he had picked a winner. Veronica Mainwaring was certainly very sensitive, the only question was, would she be strong enough? Trance work was a dreadful strain, it always told heavily on the men who acted as the occult telephone when the lodges were communicating. She would probably last his time, however; all he wanted was the Words of Power. Things certainly seemed propitious; at any rate, he would have a look at his horoscope and see what foreboded.

Lucas knew from experience the influence of the macrocosm which is our universe, upon the microcosm which is man, and he would not, if it could be avoided, embark upon an enterprise of such importance as the present if the stars were unpropitious.

'True, a man can master his stars,' he would say, 'but why should I swim against the current when, if I but wait a little while, the tide will be with me?' So he noted the set of the heavenly tides and so ordered his course that they might aid and not oppose.

What he found tonight was quite satisfactory. Neptune, the occult planet, was well aspected in his House of Fortune, reinforced by Mars, the fighter; the only doubtful aspect was Venus, much afflicted, and in the House of Death.

Lucas considered the chart carefully. 'Ah, well,' he said finally, 'one cannot have everything, and anyway, Venus is not a lady who has ever troubled me much.' With which he too went to bed.

Veronica did not think that the Ashlotts would be stirring much before seven. She set her alarm for five o'clock, that would give her time to pack her scanty belongings into the two suitcases that constituted her luggage, and enable her to slip round to the hostel before anybody in this house was stirring. The superintendent had been uneasy at the time she had accepted the post, and would surely lend assistance, even if Veronica judiciously suppressed the inci-

30

dent of the collar and chain, which was likely to invalidate her whole story, prime horror though it was. The fact that Lucas had chased her downstairs and forcibly prevented her from leaving the house was quite sufficient.

She fell into an uneasy doze, between sleeping and waking, but whenever unconsciousness stole over her she was snatched back by fear, and wide awake, every nerve tingling, every muscle taut, her whole soul stood upon the defensive.

It seemed but a little while before grey stole into the sky, and as soon as it was light enough to see, she arose and packed. It was before six o'clock that she stole on tip-toe down the passage; there was no Lucas on the settee this time, as she had almost expected to see him, and her progress was unbarred.

She crept on and on with her heart in her mouth; she knew the Ashlotts slept in the basement, but she was not sure where Lucas's room was.

The hall was filled with the stale odours of a shut-up house, but the great front door presented no difficulties, its bolts were never shot, a spring lock alone securing the house from intrusion, for Mrs Ashlott's 'gentlemen' came and went at all hours of the twenty-four. It opened silently, but Veronica did not dare to risk the click of the lock should she shut it behind her. For a moment she paused on the broad step, was that strange chain going to tighten and strangle her? Nothing happened, however, and in another moment she was speeding down the street – free!

In five minutes she was round at the hostel, where the superintendent, clad in a wrapper but wide awake, viewed her with surprise mingled with disapproval.

'What brings you here at this time in the morning?' she demanded.

Veronica was almost too breathless to reply, and the superintendent, seeing that trouble was afoot, drew her into the office out of the gaze of an inquisitive charwoman. There, she turned gimlet eyes upon the girl and awaited her explanation. The world is very ready with advice and warning to save the young and innocent from getting into difficulties, but once trouble has supervened it is a different matter, and the world begins to think how best it can avoid being involved.

'There has been,' began Veronica awkwardly, 'a little unpleasantness where I have been working. Mr Lucas, the man I am working for ... I think he forgot himself ... we had a scuffle ... I don't want to go back again. Can I stop here? Is my room still empty?'

'Your room is not let yet,' said the superintendent somewhat ungraciously. 'Yes, I suppose you can stop here if you want to, so long as there is not further trouble, but we don't want any unpleasantness here. I will send the porter round for your box. I thought at the time you were very ill-advised to take that post.'

She paused, eyeing Veronica inquisitively. 'What is Mr Lucas like?' she inquired finally.

'He is a very strange man,' began Veronica slowly, 'the strangest I have ever met.' Memory called up a vision of Lucas before her eyes. Smooth olive skin, sharp-cut nose, thin lipped, firm of chin, with the uncanny greeny-brown eyes. What would he do when he found she had got away? She paused, oblivious of the superintendent, arrested by the image that rose so vividly before her eyes. But horror of horrors – it was ceasing to be a memory-picture, it was becoming alive, actual, capable of action! A thin brown hand was being stretched out towards her as it had been the night before, a voice (surely the superintendent must hear it?) was saying: 'There is a steel collar about your neck, you will not be able to breathe if you say any more. There is a steel chain attached to the collar, the end of it is in my hand, you will have to come back.' Jerk. Veronica took two stumbling steps towards the door. Another jerk at the chain, and she took two more.

'Where are you going?' demanded the superintendent, staring at her suspiciously.

'I – I have changed my mind,' said Veronica, 'I shall have to go back after all.'

The superintendent snorted. 'You need not come here again if you do,' she said; and shut the door in the girl's face.

Veronica, on the doorstep, realized that her sole refuge was now closed to her, she was more in Lucas's hands than ever. She had lost her purse in the scuffle on the stairs, and it only contained a few shillings had she had it; there was nothing for her to do, apart from the pressure of the steel chain, but to go back to the house in the square. So back she went.

Mrs Ashlott was cleaning the steps when she arrived, so she was spared the ordeal of ringing the bell.

'Been for an early morning walk?' asked the good woman, a smile on her pleasant face. 'I like to see young ladies who can get up early, so few can nowadays, not like when I was a girl. I will soon have your breakfast up, Miss, I expect you are hungry.'

Veronica was too near tears to answer her; she slipped past the bucket and crept upstairs.

Back in her room, Veronica flung herself on her bed and fell into a dead sleep, from which she was roused by the sounds of Mrs Ashlott laying the table in the next room.

Veronica ate her breakfast and reviewed the situation. She was absolutely penniless; she had estranged the superintendent of the hostel by her inexplicable behaviour; Lucas had her more completely in his hands than ever, had that been possible.

That good man, singing lustily to the accompaniment of running bath-water, was feeling very well content with life; and indeed he had no reason to be otherwise.

Veronica, awaiting his pleasure at ten o'clock, was informed that she looked as if she had spent a night on the tiles, and had better go for a walk in Regent's Park and get freshened up.

'On a lead, of course,' he added with a mischievous

smile. 'But if you are good, as I think you will be, you shall have a nice blue bow on your collar, and how would you like a bell? Wouldn't you like a bell on your collar, Miss Mainwaring?'

Veronica beat a hasty retreat. One of the horrors of Lucas's personality was the pleasant way in which he did unspeakable things; that, and his eyes – his eyes when the pupils contracted to pinpoints. Veronica had not had very much experience of life. For her, villains were villains and looked the part, and Lucas, though he was dark, which is one of the principal qualifications for villainship, did not look a villain. Neither did he behave like one, except at the melodramatic moment when he chased her downstairs, but his subsequent nonchalance had almost annulled the impression.

Veronica returned from her walk to find a message from Lucas awaiting her; she was to go and lie down and have a good sleep, as he would be needing her that evening and wanted her to be fresh. The second half of the message was quite sufficient to render the first half impossible. She went to her room, but not to sleep; instead, she tossed backwards and forwards on her bed wondering what demands were about to be made upon her.

Veronica was young in years, and young for her years. From the time she left school till the break-up of her home, she and her mother had lived in a little cottage in a Surrey village. The garden, the church, an occasional tea party with women who led lives as limited as their own, had not tended to broaden her outlook.

Hers was naturally a sweet nature; gentle, because she had never had need of anything but gentleness; and affectionate. She had been trained in the Christian virtues, but she had had no training for life as it is lived beyond the confines of their quiet village.

Now, in Lucas's hands she was helpless. She did not

34

know what to do or where to turn. After her rebuff by the superintendent, Veronica's resources were exhausted. Lucas horrified her, but at the same time fascinated her. She knew nothing of the psychology of suggestion, or the subtle reactions that sex makes under hypnosis; all she knew was that Lucas's power over her had an element of fascination about it that she could not explain even to herself.

As the time drew near for her to face Lucas, she changed her tumbled jumper and skirt for a little grey frock, a frock that had not seen the light of day since the last tea party under the tree in that Surrey garden. Wavy brown hair was brushed and bound with a ribbon, and though her eyes were heavy because she had cried, she was a very different girl to the thin and haggard creature who had first come to the house.

At nine o'clock Lucas sent Ashlott up to fetch her, and with her heart beating uncomfortably in her throat, she followed him down the thickly-carpeted stairs to the room, half office, half study, where Lucas spent his days. There she found him, smoking an after-dinner pipe, which he waved cheerfully at her on her entry. He was very wide awake and well pleased with life; Veronica had already observed that he always seemed to wake up towards evening, but tonight he seemed extra wide awake. Silently she took the seat he assigned to her in an enormous armchair which completely engulfed her small person, and looked up at Lucas as he stood before her, nursing his pipe and studying her quizzically.

'Have you been a good child and had your sleep?' he demanded.

Veronica, in a small voice, replied that she had.

'That's right. I have told Ashlott that we are not to be disturbed, but we may as well lock the door. No, you needn't look at me like that, I am not going to murder you, but if anyone wakes you up suddenly when you are in a trance it gives you a nasty shock.'

35

He walked across the room and turned the key, then knocked the ashes out of his pipe and put it away. Veronica, motionless, as if bound to her chair, watched every moment he made with that eerie fascination he always had for her. His quick, silent step, his alert yet graceful carriage, were unlike those of any man she had ever seen before. Lucas was so very much alive that he made every other being seem devitalized, flat, and stale. The green eyes with their strange gleams, the slender student's hands with their long brown fingers, the crow-black hair that he rubbed up on end when he was puzzled, the neat, thin-lipped mouth that always seemed to be enjoying some quiet joke at her expense in which the eyes never joined – all these gave the girl an intense and vivid sense of the man's personality. Lucas, if it had not been for his eyes, would have given the impression of being a pleasant enough fellow, but there was something wrong with the eyes; a kind of detachment, as if he did not belong to the human world. Veronica, watching him, knew that appeals for human mercy would have no meaning for him.

Lucas fidgeted about the room, apparently waiting for the sunset, Veronica's eyes following him. Then as the last light died, he came over to Veronica. He dropped on one knee in front of her, bringing his keen dark face on a level with hers.

'Look straight into my eyes, Miss Mainwaring,' he said.

Veronica, horrified but fascinated, looked as bidden, and saw that the pupils were pulsating with a strange inner light, as if Lucas's skull contained, not brains, but a blazing fire that shone out through the lens of the eyeballs. Once she had met those eyes, she was powerless to withdraw her own. The blaze grew brighter and brighter, the man's face disappeared, and she was gazing straight into the furnace of which his form was but the screen. She seemed to be passing through the flames into that which lay beyond. Then, suddenly, the ground went from under her feet, and she plunged downwards into illimitable blue-blackness; out be-

36

tween the planets she seemed to fall into stellar space. Then the curve of her course turned upwards as a diver returns to the surface, the blue grew lighter, it was the pale sapphire that precedes the sunrise. Back she came through rosy dawn clouds, and woke up in her chair.

Lucas stood before her in his shirt sleeves. The twilight was still coming in through the window, but the green student's lamp was lighted.

'Well?' he said, 'safely back again. Not so very bad, was it?'

Except for the awful swoop into space, Veronica could not honestly say that it had been bad, and admitted as much.

Lucas heaved a sigh of relief, which ended in a yawn, stretched himself, and walked abou the room as if to relieve cramped limbs. A little cold wind blew in through the window and stirred a great pile of manuscript in Lucas's handwriting that lay upon the desk. Veronica wondered where he had got it from, it had not been there when she had closed her eyes a few moments before. The cold air from without made Lucas shiver, and he picked up his coat that lay on the floor and slid himself into it. The action made Veronica realize that she, too, was cold, perishingly cold, as if with the chill of outer space, and a convulsive shudder ran through her. Lucas smiled as if he had been watching for this to happen, and took up a small vacuum flask that stood upon the desk. A curl of steam ascended into the air as he unscrewed the cover.

'Cold?' he said. 'You always are after a trance. Have some hot coffee,' and he poured the contents of the flask into a cup that stood ready to hand.

Veronica sipped her coffee. She noticed that the light in the room was getting brighter, though the student's lamp on the desk was looking palid and unwholesome. The brightening light was coming from the window. A twitter and rustle from the ivy announced that the sparrows were rousing; Veronica, bewildered, wondered what could have disturbed them at that hour of the night. Lucas switched off the lamp on the desk, and Veronica saw that the room was full of a cold grey light, twilight indeed, but the growing, not the waning, twilight, and she suddenly realized that in some peculiar way, seven hours had vanished out of her life. She had passed from the twilight of night to the twilight of dawn, and what had been done to her in that interval she would never know. There was Lucas, looking very tired but quite ordinary and matter of fact; there was that great pile of manuscript, evidently written during those seven hours, but of whose nature she was ignorant.

She looked fixedly at Lucas, as if she would drag the truth from him by the very intensity of her gaze.

'What happened while I – was asleep?'

'You went out.'

'Out. What do you mean?'

'Out of your body. Your soul went out of your body. I pushed you out.'

'But why. What for?'

'Because I wanted to use your body as a telephone. When you are in your body, the impulses of your mind control the vocal cords, and you speak; but if you are out of your body, the impulses of other people's minds can be made to control your vocal cords, and they speak. Do you know any German? No? Well, you have been talking it fluently all night and told me a lot of things I wanted to know. That is why you are useful to me, little girl, and that is why I want to keep you. You can go about and have as good a time as you like, provided you do not impair your sensitiveness, but you must not go away.' He came close up to her and gazed deeply and fixedly into her eyes. 'You can go just the length of your chain, but not further. Understand?'

Veronica recieved his explanation without grasping its import. It was so much beyond the sphere of her concepts that it conveyed very little to her. She realized that Lucas made some curious use of her, that he set a good deal of

38

value on her as an instrument, and that she would be kept, as a domestic animal is kept, under the best conditions, but for the uses of its master. Horror and fear overcame her; the whole transaction was not human; Lucas was not regarding her as a human being, but as a tool or instrument; the purposes for which he was using her were not human purposes, motivated by lust or greed, but some ultra-human or infra-human aim, altogether outside the scope of our earth-life. What he was trying to do, she did not know, but she was certain he was damaging her soul; in spite of his pleasantness and agreeableness he was hurting her in some way that was not physical, but that was doing her infinitely more harm than anything done to her body ever could have done. She was afraid with a cold and deadly fear, a fear not of the body, but of the soul; a fear, not of our earth, with its human wickedness, but of outer space and the things that are not human. Lucas himself was not quite human. Sitting there on the office table, swinging his legs and drinking beer out of a tea-cup, he looked more than human, he looked positively ordinary, but she knew that he was not. She stared at him intently, trying to solve the riddle; what was it about him that was not human? It was his hands, his eyes, and, funnily enough, his feet. Veronica could not make out why she included his feet in her inventory, but she did.

Looking up, he met her gaze and smiled at her over the tea-cup.

'Go to bed, Miss Mainwaring,' he said.

'I am not sleepy,' she replied.

'Of course, I forgot. You have had seven hours double-distilled sleep. I am, though, if you are not, so I will bid you good night, or good morning, whichever you prefer.'

CHAPTER FOUR

Veronica found that, from the mundane point of view, her life was an easy one. There was no drudgery over typewriting or book-keeping; all day she could do as she pleased, read, sew, knit jumpers, walk in the park, go to a cinema, anything, in fact, so long as she did not over-tire herself, for that made Lucas very cross indeed.

Three or four nights a week Ashlott would bring a message to say that she was wanted in the office, and then Lucas, gazing deeply into her eyes, would push her soul out into space and use her body for his own purposes. At dawn she would return to the vacated tenement, frightened, dazed, and utterly cold. Never again, however, did she experience the complete loss of memory that had occurred on the occasion of her first trance. Shreds of consciousness carried over; sometimes she would be aware of faces that moped and mowed at her as she swept on the downward curve of her arc, and, like a frightened bird, she would round the nadir and speed upwards to the dawn clouds. Upon one terrible, never-to-be-forgotten night, they had chased her through inter-planetary space, and she had woken up, long before her appointed time, shrieking with terror, to find Lucas, half angry, half alarmed, holding her down in her chair. She had told him of the fiend faces and clawing hands that had pursued her, but he merely shrugged his shoulders and offered no comment or explanation, though she noticed that it was some time before he summoned her again.

She had been three weeks in that strange house, and a sultry August had changed into a burning September, when Lucas came to her with a key in his hand.

'A pity I never thought of it before, but here is the key of the Square gardens, you can go and sit there in the evenings while I am away. I am getting off for the week-end,' he added.

A little later she saw him in motor-bike kit, and guessed that his holiday would be spent on the open road. Wistfully she thought of clear wind-swept spaces and fresh air. Bloomsbury, never a very cheerful part of London, is the most intolerable, cat-haunted vacancy in the summer. Veronica went over to the Square and sat under the trees. The gardens were a godsend; though parched and faded, there was some green left, and at any rate she was not between four walls.

Meanwhile, Lucas, having cleared the London traffic, was speeding North at a good pace. He, too, was rejoicing in freedom from bricks and mortar. It was a long while since he had had his motor-bike out; the amount of time he was spending over Veronica Mainwaring and the results he was obtaining from her made it necessary for him to employ the week-ends in catching up with his regular work. But it was worth it, such a medium was not to be met with every day. Clear as a bell, the messages came through, and he was getting them co-ordinated; bit by bit he was piecing together the rituals of the higher degrees of the great Fraternity to which he belonged. Lucas chuckled as he thought of what his private safe contained.

The wind of his speed sang in his ears, and his blood sang, too, for he was a man, and young, and even his whole-hearted absorption in his occult studies had not deprived him of his manhood. Sometimes he wondered if it were worth it, this ascetic strictness of discipline, this sacrifice of the things that made life worth living for most men. Ahead of him and behind him were other motor-bikes, some with a girl on the carrier. Lucas had never taken a girl on his

41

carrier; one of the brethren, perhaps, who happened to be in a hurry, but a girl, never. Women did not come into his life. The Order to which he belonged did not admit them, and the few women he had known in his journalistic days had slipped out of his life when he joined the Order.

He stopped for tea at a wayside inn. In the bay window of the parlour a young man and a girl were eating eggs and watercress and chaffing each other. Lucas was no hermit. Unless his skin lied, there was Latin blood in him, and his temperament had the quick liveliness of the South. He watched the couple and felt out of it. For the first time since he had escaped from the turgid 'teens, he considered a woman attentively. It might be rather amusing to take a girl out. Of course, he had his work to do, nothing could be allowed to interfere with that, but why should he cut himself off from all the pleasant things of life? Why should he work like a galley-slave to win power and independence when by the time he had obtained them he would be too old and too inured to his solitude to be able to enjoy them? Lucas finished his tea thoughtfully; a new idea had been presented to him, and he was assessing it. What would be the effect upon his life if he admitted to it that neglected factor? Trained to absolute self-control by the great Fraternity whose pupil and servant he was, he had had little difficulty in banishing from his life women and all the tangled problems they presented. Completely possessed, body and soul, by his absorbing studies, he had hardly missed them, or realized how much his life deviated from the normal. But into his seclusion he had introduced a disturbing element. Veronica Mainwaring when he first saw her, haggard, shabby, and weary, had not been an object of allurement; indeed, he had regarded her impersonally, looking upon her simply as an instrument to serve his ends, like typewriter and telephone. But Veronica, unluckily for her, had not remained as she was when she entered the big house in the Square; Lucas, in order to ensure her efficiency, had had her fed and cared for, and the result had shown on other planes than the psychic one. The dull skin had cleared, the heavy eyes had brightened, and the frail figure had filled out surprisingly quickly. And with the return of vitality a change had come in her spiritual quality; the life in her now began to overflow in subtle vibrations that Lucas, quick to sense an atmosphere, had become aware of.

Veronica, who regarded Lucas as a bird regards a cat, had exercised upon him none of the feminine arts that come so readily to the least sophisticated of women, but the pressure of the race behind her had flowed out, and Lucas, who had so carefully guarded himself from all calls of the race, found the tide about his feet before he was aware of its existence for him.

Veronica's presence intensified his self-consciousness, caused the pressure of his vitality to rise; life appeared in more vivid colours when she was present; she was a stimulus to him, and deprived of her life felt stale, flat, and unprofitable.

All this was not present to the man's consciousness, however, as he wheeled the heavy bike into the roadway and stood debating. All he realized was that he was missing something which appeared to be amusing, and was wondering whether it was worth the trouble of obtaining. But Nature is an old and subtle woman, jealous of her own way, and she did not reveal to him the meaning of the call that sounded in his ears. It is not her will that any of her children should break from their allegiance.

Occult power can be obtained in two ways, by placing oneself in the van of evolution, where force has not yet been confined in form but lies loose, as it were, free to enter whatever channel is opened to it; or by retreating to the rear of the race, where unabsorbed force is again available. Lucas had chosen the latter path; he, with all the endowments of modern humanity, had deliberately reverted to an earlier phase of evolution, to a time when space was void and forms were being built. Lucas, the non-social, the solitary, and therefore the free, was being drawn into the current of evolution. He who had set out to master his race and was well on the road to accomplishment was a Samson shorn of his locks. His source of strength had been his complete freedom from all sense of obligation to his kind, and therefore from scruple or remorse, which naturally placed him at a great advantage in dealing with men who were subject to both.

It was the beginning of the end, had he known it, when he wheeled his cycle out into the road with the handle-bars to the South. Nature had caught Lucas.

That day, for the first time since he had left his boyhood behind him. Lucas had had a thought that did not centre about his own ego – he had handed the key of the gardens to Veronica, and thereby Nature had noosed him, for when a man says to evil, 'Be thou my good,' he can own no divided allegiance, for his god is the most jealous of all the gods, and his own human nature will betray him should one thought stray from its dark loyalty. It is only the very strong who can hope to swim against the current of the universe.

The sun had set, and the glow over the London chimney pots was failing, but Veronica still sat on in the shabby garden of the Bloomsbury Square. She had not sat under a tree since she had left the little Surrey village that now seemed like some dim memory of another existence. She was languid and apathetic; the air, stale and heavy, hung about her without movement; her mind was almost a blank, for Lucas's operations had tended to slow her mental processes, and, although a background of fear still remained, she no longer planned escape. She felt herself to be helpless, completely under Lucas's control, and she had no thought of defying her gaoler, but merely a dim hope that his will might alleviate her lot, and that he would not lay upon her burdens too great to be borne.

She did not perceive a man who stood behind the railings, watching her through the scanty privet hedge that enclosed the gardens. Locked up in her own thoughts, the London square had faded, and she was back again on the Surrey hills. Her old daydreams were rising before her mind in little pictures; the Prince Charming, who had never appeared, was evoked from his palace in the clouds and set to his task of dragon-slaying (the dragon being Lucas), and then she would fly away, as with the wings of a dove, and be at peace. No castle in the clouds did she construct for herself, the Surrey hills were good enough for her tired little soul; the rambler roses, the pear trees, and the tall blue lupins of her little garden, with the old servant, half nurse half housekeeper, to give her her tea, and the cat purring on the rag mat before the kitchen hearth. Meanwhile, the man watched her through the railings.

She arose, gathered up her forgotten needlework, and moved slowly over the deadened grass towards the gate; the stale twilight had turned to the hot airlessness of a city night, and the arc-lamps at the corner of the square deprived even the darkness of its relief. As she reached the gate she became aware that she was looking into a pair of eyes; to her, moving in a waking dream, they seemed just eyes, independent of any face in which they might be set, till a voice broke upon her reverie.

'The gate is locked, you will have to unlock it before you can get out.' And she found herself face to face with Lucas.

She returned to waking life with a shock. The search for the key gave her an excuse to withdraw her eyes from Lucas's, a thing she found difficult to do when once she had looked into them, for she was always watching for the change to take place in the pupils, thankful for every moment that they remained normal. The rusty lock yielded reluctantly to her efforts and she stood beside the man on the pavement. They walked across the road without speaking. Lucas seemed absorbed in thought, but the girl had a notion that he was watching her covertly. In unbroken silence he admitted her with his latch key, and switched on the light in the darkened hall. Without glancing at him she made straight for the stairs, throwing him a little nervous good night over her shoulder, to which he did not reply. As she turned to ascend the second flight she saw that he was still watching her, standing where she had left him, face and clothes grey with the dust of the road. She hastened her steps into the sheltering darkness of the upper floors, thankful to escape from this disturbing scrutiny. Why had he returned so unexpectedly? Why did he look at her in this peculiar way, as if he had never seen her before? To neither question could she find an answer; the uncertainty was not reassuring, and dawn was grey before she fell into an uneasy sleep.

She was finishing a belated breakfast on Sunday morning when the door opened and Lucas announced himself.

'I should recommend you,' he said, 'to put on something ancient in the way of a skirt, and then, if you are a good girl, I will take you for a little jaunt.'

Veronica stared at him uncomprehendingly; what new psychic experiment was this he contemplated? He surveyed her with an amused smile.

'Don't you think we deserve a little holiday?' he said. 'Have you ever ridden on the pillion of a motor-bike? It's great fun. I thought we would run down to Brighton for lunch, listen to a concert or something, and come back in the cool of the evening.'

Veronica continued to stare at him without reply, and the man's face darkened.

'What do you imagine I intend to do with you, cut your throat?' he asked, sharply.

'Oh, no,' replied Veronica, 'I – just didn't quite understand.'

'Well, you understand now, so go and get your things on,' he said, and turning on his heel, left the room.

He was oppressed by a sense that something was not quite right. This was not the way in which the little expe-

46

dition should have started; and when Veronica, leaden-footed, reluctant, descended the stairs ten minutes later, his oppression deepened. In unbroken silence she perched herself upon the carrier according to his instructions, but twice she had to be told to grip the leather belt that encircled his waist.

'If you don't hold on, you'll fall off round the first corner,' he said angrily, starting the machine off with a jerk that enforced his commands. Veronica clutched him frantically and shut her eyes as they shot into the traffic of the main road.

The silence was unbroken till they had left London behind and were racing southwards towards the coast.

'How do you like it?' he called back over his shoulder to the girl behind him, but she, the wind of their speed singing in her ears, did not hear him. He, however, thought her silence was deliberate, and sent the machine flying down a slope, exhaust roaring, as if he meant to drive the pair of them to eternity.

At the bottom he stopped the machine, slipped out of the saddle, and stood in the roadway facing Veronica, his eyes blazing.

'Is this the way you mean to behave?' he said.

Veronica stared back at him. This was a different Lucas to the one she had encountered before, and one that she was not in the least afraid of. This one was human.

'I don't know what you mean,' she said.

'I mean – are you going to sulk all day?'

Veronica looked up at the branches that met over their heads, and at the blue sky beyond them. She had no hope, her last refuge was gone, and, strangely enough, her fear was gone with it.

'I don't care what you do,' she said. 'You can do anything you like, and if you killed me, I shouldn't mind.'

'Do you dislike me?'

'Yes.'

'Why?'

'Because of what you do to me. I can't put it into words, but you know quite well what I mean.'

'What do I do to you?'

'I don't know. I don't know what you do to me, but it is all wrong, you have no right to do what you are doing.'

'But you don't know why I am doing it.'

She looked at him in surprise, the tone was one she had never heard him use before.

'Listen, Veronica, I am after a big thing, so big you couldn't understand it; it means everything to me, and this is the only way in which I can do it. Stand by me, see it through, and I swear you shall never regret it.'

This was indeed a reversal of their positions. Lucas the aloof, Lucas the autocrat, pleading for something that it was in her power to give or withhold! Why did her mind work so slowly? She could not reply to him.

Then the man spoke again. 'Listen, and I will tell you what I am after. I am after knowledge, Veronica. Knowledge that I can alter the world with. If I get that knowledge, I should be able to make the nations put aside their armaments, I could make the legislatures put through social reforms, I could do all these things, I have already done bits of them – and the fools who hold this knowledge make no use of it and they won't let me have it. That is why I am stealing it, Veronica, because I can make use of it, and they can't.'

'I don't know what you are talking about, Mr Lucas,' said Veronica, 'and I don't know what it is that you want, but I think they are quite right not to let you have it. I wouldn't trust you with anything.'

Lucas gasped. His was at no time a personality to be lightly set aside, and this attack, coming from little Veronica who always crept about like a mouse, took his breath away.

'What do you mean? Why wouldn't you trust me? What have I done to you to make you say that?'

'I don't know what you are doing to me, but you know;

and I know it is harmful, and you know it, too. But you think because I can't say it in so many words exactly what it is you are up to, that I don't suspect anything.'

'What do you mean. How much do you know?'

'I don't know anything. I don't pretend to know anything, but I feel things, and I feel that you are not one of us.'

'Many a true word spoken in ignorance. And if I am not one of you, what may I be?'

'I don't know what you may be. I only know that you are different. If I said to any other man "You are hurting me," he would stop, but if I said it to you, you would only say "Don't make a noise." You don't feel about things as we do. I think you are going a different way.'

Lucas looked out into the shadowy spaces of the wood with unseeing eyes. There was a long pause.

'Yes, that is just about it. I am going a different way, and I'm damned lonely. I had never realized it before. That is what has been the matter all the time. There is not one solitary human being who would understand what I am driving at, whom I could talk things over with. I am going absolutely alone. And even if one is on the left-hand path, one likes companionship. And by God, I'll have it!' He caught Veronica by the arm. 'You're coming, too, Veronica. There are possibilities in you. Your nature is so simple it is almost primitive. I'll push you back to Pan. I'll put you on the Green Ray. You with the pale nature-green, I with the dark occult-green, we should have the complete Green Ray between us. Veronica, will you come? It means power, it means life. Not the cooped-up existence of civilization, but free, as the pagans lived!'

The man's face was alight, pupils distended into pools of gleaming blackness, a flush under the dark skin. Veronica looked back into those eyes, and, as ever, their fascination drew her; but now there was no sense of horror, just a pouring forth of power that quickened the life within her, causing it to flow forth in response to him. As he spoke, the green forest twilight seemed to be rayed with gleams of gold; it was no longer a shadowed green, but a glowing green. A faint airy piping, as of little pipes in the air, came to her ears, half heard, half dreamed. Was it the image aroused by the name of Pan that made her think these things? Something naked, non-human, but alive as no human being ever is alive, slipped from bush to bush behind her, edging nearer and nearer; the little pipes sounded clearer; a patter as of small, sharp hoofs was upon the fallen leaves, and the light was shot through with green gleams like the fire in an opal. Something was almost at her elbow, and it was calling to her, calling, calling, and in another minute she would have gone: following it into the greenwood to come back nevermore, for the fairies would have taken her. What was that old story told by her nurse of the children the fairies stole if their cradles were left unguarded? And that was why children had to be christened, so that the fairies could not steal them. But she had been christened, the fairies could not steal her. What were these little Pan-things plucking at her skirts? They were not her kind. She had nothing to do with them. She had been christened. She had been taught her prayers. She saw herself kneeling on the rag mat in front of the kitchen fire saying them to her old nurse. She remembered learning her very first prayer, it began, 'Gentle Jesus, meek and mild, Look upon a little child.'

With a gasp, as of a swimmer returning to the surface, Veronica found herself standing in the middle of the road. There was hard road, dusty road, under her feet, and above her head were trees, their first leaves falling with the drought. Before her stood a man, and his face was a queer grey, and sweat stood out on his forehead.

'Hold this,' he said, and thrusting the heavy bike into her hands, he staggered across to the bank at the side of the road, and dropped down on it, hiding his face in his hands.

Veronica stood helplessly, holding the cumbersome machine and marvelling what could have happened to

50

Lucas, he looked as if he had had a bad shock of some sort. She herself felt singularly steady, and her mind was clearer than it had been for a long time. It seemed as if her faculties, sinking into abeyance since Lucas had commenced his work, had returned to her.

Presently he raised his head and looked at her.

'I didn't know you were under protection,' he said. 'It is the first time you have ever shown any signs of it.'

He rose, and somewhat unsteadily came across and took the machine from her, fixing it upon its stand.

'Come and sit down,' he said, leading her over to the grass at the road side. 'We will go on presently.'

For a long while they sat in silence, and then Lucas said, without looking at her: 'Do you know what it was you did to me?'

Veronica shook her head.

'No, you don't know anything, do you? All the same, I have got a pretty shrewd suspicion that you know a good deal more than you know you know.'

Silence fell again between them.

Then the man spoke once more, still never looking at her.

'I am going to tell you a story. There was a man in Rome, ancient Rome, who, as a boy, had lived at his uncle's villa outside the walls because he was an orphan. He was affianced to his cousin, a girl much younger than he; and, although his life had a dark side to it, he always returned to the villa outside the walls, for he cared for that girl very much, more than she was old enough to understand, for they married them young in those days. He was a student of the Mysteries, and one day he went away to Eleusis to take his initiation, expecting that when he came back they would be married. On his return, he found that she had become a Christian, and, taught by her new doctrines, considered him a bad man, and would not marry him.

'So the best thing in his life went out of it, the thing that had been his sheet-anchor, and he turned to the dark side of

51

the Mysteries. He said to Evil, be thou my good, and Evil took him at his word.'

Silence fell again. Veronica broke it this time.

'What became of her?' she said.

'There were no nuns in those days, or she would have become one, but she ministered to the poor Christians and saved many souls. But she didn't save his, she lost that. You owe me a debt, Veronica.'

CHAPTER FIVE

It was some little while before Lucas was sufficiently re-covered to make a move, and even then his nerve seemed to be shaken, for he drove with much more caution than was his wont. As it was, they arrived at Brighton later than they had intended, and finished a belated lunch only just in time for them to go on the pier and find seats for the concert.

From where they sat they could see the steamers on the horizon, all the busy shipping of the English Channel, the most populous water-highway in the world; Lucas, hardly listening to the music, watched the shadowy procession of sea-power with unseeing eyes. The girl at his side, as a physical entity, was forgotten, he conceived of her only as a soul, voyaging through time towards some goal of her own choosing, her feet set upon a path from which he had failed to deflect her. She was following the way of her race; a flock of sheep in a gully, was the simile that always rose to his mind when he thought of that well-worn path staked out by the creeds of his countrymen; foolish eyes fixed on the woolly back just in front, and patient little hoofs going patter, patter, patter over the rough track that ended at the slaughter house. As for him, he was a goat of Ishmael's flock, free upon the mountains with his Dark Master. Yet, when he sought to cut out his little chosen ewe-lamb from the herd below, a great Crook had struck him back.

What was this power that intervened? He was familiar enough with the punitive rays the Order could employ upon occasion, but this was of a different type of force, it was

53

unfamiliar to him. It shook his nerve, making him feel uncertain of his path, doubtful of his goal. He stole a glance at the girl who sat beside him; she had the soft round face so common among English girls, but there was upon it an expression that was not common, the calm of absolute repose. The face was still as is the face of one just aroused from deep sleep; the strained, haunted look that had become habitual to her during the past weeks was wiped out, and in its place was a great peace; some power had passed and left its mark upon her. He studied the face intently, trying to divine its secret. Veronica, he knew, could tell him nothing, however much he questioned her, not because she would not, but because she could not put her thoughts into words. She was of the feeling type, not the reasoning type.

The man withdrew his eyes from her face and re-pondered the problem. She was an ideal tool, too good to be lost, but a hitch had occurred in the handling of her. Suddenly, at a time when he believed her to be completely subject to his will, there had come through her one of the rushes of unseen force with which those who traffic in occult things are familiar, and Lucas had been knocked out as a boxer is knocked out when hit on the solar plexus.

He knew quite well what that meant. Like all students of the hidden side of things, he was a believer in reincarnation, and he held that each soul that aspires finds its way sooner or later into one or other of the great occult fraternities; then, life after life, it always returns to the shadow of that fraternity, for 'once an Initiate, always an Initiate', and just as he could have availed himself of the power latent in his Fraternity, so Veronica, in her moment of danger, had found a force overshadowing her, and it was a force with which he was unfamiliar. He cast his mind backwards into the past, seeking some clue that might enlighten him. Like all occultists of a certain degree of initiation, he could remember his past lives as other men remember their childhood, dim and far away, but none the less tangible; and though, like a child, he might remember people whom he

54

had met in those far off days, he did not always recognize them when they reappeared under their present guise.

He cursed himself for not realizing that something more than rational judgement must have been at work when, out of a whole roomful of women he chose one, and one only, for use in his dangerous adventure.

He had often lived over again in memory that Roman life of his: seen the white villa and talked with the gentle girl who dwelt in it, and passing from that life back along the chain of memory, seen other lives where they, priest and priestess, had borne their part in the mysteries of many climes and ages, right back to the dim dawn of knowledge in the sun-worship of ancient Atlantis. Undoubtedly the bond had held age after age, and such a bond as that is not a thing to be ignored; the causes it had set going would actuate events in the present life to an extent undreamed of by the ordinary man; if he could estimate those forces he would be able to form a very fair idea of the conditions he would have to cope with in working out this problem, and he cursed himself again that his knowledge had not enabled him to avoid involving himself in such a Karmic tangle. Here he was, half-way thorugh a most critical and vital experiment, and the forces of a forgotten Roman summer had wakened to life again and threatened to complicate the whole affair.

Lucas brought his mind forward, life by life, from the remote past to the immediate present, striving to see the course events had taken in past lives so that he might be able to deduce their tendency. He had not recognized in Veronica the presence of the soul whose orbit he had repeatedly touched. That soul had had an element of greatness in it, and there was nothing big about Veronica, she was more of a child than anything else.

Lucas stirred impatiently in his chair. If she had been the woman who had worked with him in the past, what a different proposition it would have been, but something had

55

gone wrong in that Roman incarnation to which he had not got the clue, and he was baffled.

He touched Veronica's arm.

'If you have heard enough music, we will have tea and start for home.'

She acquiesced, passive and unresponsive as ever, and they, or rather he, for she took no part in the quest, sought out a tea-shop. She irritated him beyond measure when she was in this mood. To attempt to bully Veronica into better behaviour would only make her lie down completely; to cheer her was impossible.

But Veronica's mind was not as passive as he thought. She was brooding deeply over the happenings in the roadway. The story he had told her, trite enough in its way, had made a deep impression, and the images it evoked rose persistently before her mind. She could see the white villa, the sub-tropical gardens, the oxen at the well-wheel, and the slaves who tilled the vine terraces, with the clear, vivid detail that she could see the Surrey cottage. Of course the girl refused her lover, what else could she have done? Their lives were going different ways, they could not walk together. But she had not forgotten him, Veronica was certain of that; no, she had remembered the dark patrician Roman as she worked among the outcasts of the city, separated from him by less than a mile, as men count space, but each facing a different way so that they never saw each other.

Had she been right to escape temptation by avoiding him? The whole temperament of that age was for those who sought righteousness to leave a too sinful world and its contamination, but might not the world, unleavened by their presence, incline to greater and greater extremes of evil? For the first time in her life, Veronica was thinking rather than feeling, and the unaccustomed experience gave her a sensation of bewilderment. She turned to Lucas, feeling that she needed the steadying of his matter-of-fact demeanour, and found the man's eyes fixed on her face.

Spontaneously, unreflectively, she asked the question fermenting in her mind.

'What was his name?'

And the answer came equally spontaneously:

'Justinian. He was called after the general his father served.'

'And hers?'

'Veronica, the same as yours. (Damn fool that I was not to spot it),' he added, under his breath.

'What became of them – afterwards?'

'He studied with some of the greatest black magicians of the age, and when his body was worn out, and it wore out pretty quickly, he took another, and went on studying. Later, he had an incarnation at Avignon during the great days of witchcraft, and was burnt in the market place there, together with a number of others.'

'Was that while she was a nun?'

'How do you know she was a nun?'

'You said so, didn't you?'

'I never said anything about it. I lost her trail after I parted from her in the garden.'

'I'm sorry. I got the idea she became a nun. But what happened to him?'

'He was burnt for witchcraft, I told you that.'

Lucas, having learnt what he wanted to know, skilfully directed her attention to other subjects.

From that day the relations between the man and the girl changed profoundly. For neither of them did the old forces waken as yet, but they stirred in their sleep. The girl found herself intuitively understanding the aims and motives of the man who had appeared so incomprehensible to her, and though her antagonism was in no way lessened, she had, to a very great extent, lost her fear of him, and the sympathy, born of understanding, was, unperceived by herself, dawning faintly in the background of her mind.

For his part, the man watched events with apprehension. Old causes, he knew, were actuating from the past, but as to when and how they might come into operation, of that he was ignorant; and he was engaged in a piece of work that would not permit of disturbance, either he must push through his investigations and finish with the trance-work before the Karma began to operate, or heaven knows what complications might not be introduced into the affair. Moreover, he was still completely ignorant as to the nature of the power that had intervened in the roadway upon Veronica's behalf.

He determined, therefore, to push on with the trance-work, and four nights in succession sent Veronica out upon her astral journeyings. He had never risked working her so hard before, but he dared not delay now that the Karma had begun to stir. Out she had to go, and if she failed to return one night, then so much the better, he would be free from the old problems for the rest of this incarnation, at any rate.

The continuous trance-work was not without its effect upon the girl itself. The strange world into which she passed when she crossed the threshold of consciousness was becoming familiar to her, and its memories were beginning to link on to normal consciousness.

Never again, after the experience in the roadway, did she go out in terror and dread, for she knew that, just beyond the portal, a Presence would meet her and remain at her side till she returned. Of the nature of that Presence she had little conception, but her attitude towards it was that of a child towards a formidable but well-loved teacher.

Whereas her first expedition into the realm of the unseen had remained an utter blank in memory, her later expeditions had become increasingly tangible. Memory, at first a thing of shreds and patches, had begun to piece itself together until the pattern of the experience became visible. She was aware that she heard great rituals being enacted, but rituals that differed vastly from her previous concept of such things, based as it was upon church services.

Though each expedition differed from another, there was a certain system which seemed to prevail in all of them. First, after voyaging through blue-black space, she would perceive a glow of light dawning in the distance, and her soul, apparently set for that point of the compass, would draw steadily nearer to it. Then she would perceive that the light proceeded from some sort of an enclosure that was guarded by a barrier, but a barrier such as she had never seen upon earth, for this wall was not stationary, but revolving, resembling nothing so much as a band-saw, and reflecting gleams of light from its swiftly-moving surface. Nothing, she felt, could have projected her soul through that whirling circle, but a great, though oftentimes very spasmodic force was exerted beneath her, and with a levering motion she was lifted up and over the barrier and dropped down upon the inner side. There, as in a dream, she found herself floating; voices, faint and far away, sounded in her ears. Then a curious thing happened. It seemed as if a tenuous silver thread connected her soul with the body left behind under Lucas's care, and down this thread the impressions received by her soul were transmitted. The words she heard stimulated a reflective activity in the vocal cords of the distant throat, and the actions of the prime mover in the ceremonial were repeated by the vacated body.

But a change had begun to come over the spirit of her dream; experience had rendered the hidden side of things less unfamiliar to her, and since the event in the roadway and the coming of the Presence, she had become increasingly self-reliant when out of her body; she was no longer a leaf blown by the winds of space, but was fast developing powers of flight of her own, and a natural curiosity led her to concentrate more and more upon the strange scenes that were enacted before her, so that, as time went on, more and more of her personality began to follow her simulacrum in its scramble over the barrier, till finally, upon the fifth night of consecutive trance, the dream-scene suddenly grew real and materialized before her eyes and she found herself standing upon a broad flagged pavement with cowled figures seated all round her, and her eyes looking straight into those of one who sat upon a raised dais behind an altar. For a long moment they stared into each other's eyes, mutually staggered by the encounter, and then, rising from his seat, the cowled figure pointed a finger at her and a strangely vibrant Word rang out across the rhythms of the ritual. Instantly there was a crash as of a thousand earthquakes; lightning, tempest, and thunder seemed let loose, with herself as the focus of their force. What appeared to be a black tidal wave caught her up and swept her away as a straw in floodtime. Gasping, drowning in the darkness, she turned her mind rather than her eyes in search of the Presence that had moved at her elbow, and instantly, as she did so, she felt herself gripped, lifted, and drawn out of the maelstrom and landed upon the bank of the flood, with a voice that boomed in her ears saying:

'Return, my daughter, and We will close the gates behind thee. Seek not to come forth again unless We summon thee.'

Down and down her soul sped in its dive from the heights, and with a crash and a gasp she shot into her body in full consciousness; behind her, something that was halfway between a guillotine and a portcullis came down with a crash, and she felt rather than saw a great Hand mark it with the Sign of the Cross.

She was flat on her back on the floor, Lucas kneeling on her chest and gripping both her wrists.

'My God,' he said, 'what strength you've got! I thought I should never have been able to hold you. What happened?'

Veronica examined her bruised wrists and, collecting her scattered wits, told him as well as she could remember, all that had occurred. As she did so, she saw his face turn ashy grey.

'Do you think the man you saw would be likely to remember your face?'

'He stared at me hard enough,' said Veronica.

'Then you must clear out of here right away and we must chance the Ashlotts gossiping.'

He paused, and then continued as if speaking to himself.

'Now what in the world am I to do with her? Can't let her go altogether, no, can't possibly do that.' Pause. 'I know, the general's fishing box. Put her there. Caretaker look after her. Deaf as a post. Do as she's told and ask no questions. She knows I act for him. Keep quiet if I pay her. What time is it? Quarter past twelve. No trains tonight. Sunday tomorrow, damn it; no trains then to that God-forsaken spot. I'll have to take her down by road. Hundred and twenty miles. Council meeting tomorrow at ten; daren't miss it.' Then he seemed to wake up. He went over to a cupboard in the corner and raking about on its lower shelf, drew out a dust-covered haversack.

'Here, Veronica, you can take as much as you can stuff into this. Get your nightgown, hair brush, and washing-tackle, enough to keep you going for a day or two. I'll send your things on after you. Now hustle.'

'But Mr Lucas, what do you mean? What are you going to do with me?'

'Don't ask questions, hurry,' and taking her by the shoulders, he almost flung her out of the room. 'Put on your warmest coat,' he called after her.

Infected by his haste, she was not many minutes in carrying out his commands, but he had already changed into his motor-bike kit and was standing in the hall impatiently awaiting her.

'Is that the thickest thing you've got?' he exclaimed at sight of the thin little wrap that had to serve her needs. 'Here, take this,' and catching up an old trench coat that always hung upon the hall stand, he thrust her into it, buttoning and buckling it about her as one dresses a child. It was dirty as only a man's macintosh is allowed to get dirty, and reeked of the strong pipe tobacco he always smoked, and Veronica, cased from heel to eyes in its stiff folds,

61

felt as if, in some strange way, the man's personality enwrapped her.

Silently she followed Lucas out of the door into the close London night, the coat heavy upon her shoulders. They walked quickly, Veronica half smothered by its weight, till they came to the mews where he kept his motor-bike. He unlocked a clumsy door and got the machine out. The roar of its starting woke the echoes and he cursed it savagely, then, bidding Veronica mount behind him, he sent the machine shooting out of the yard almost before she had got her balance. Through the wide emptiness of the night streets they flew, and in an incredibly short time Veronica felt fresh air in her face and saw the loom of Harrow on its hill upon her left.

The wind blew fresh as they cleared the brick-ridden city, and when they got into the hills it cut like a knife.

On and on they went, the open exhaust roaring at Veronica's ankles and the inequalities of the road jarring the very soul out of her. Presently the darkness began to thin, the loom of objects showed up at greater and greater distance, and Lucas switched off the headlight, driving through a ghostly twilight that had something strangely unwholesome about it.

The risen sun found them upon the top of a hill with a mist-blanketed valley lying below them. For the first time since they had started upon their wild ride, Lucas broke silence.

'That's Beckering,' he said, as they slid down through thick woods towards the bottom.

They passed through a straggling village, not yet astir, and crossed a broad but shallow river by a hump-backed bridge; then, turning off down a rutted side road, they followed the windings of the river bank for close upon a mile. Thick, neglected woods closed in upon them, and the uncared-for bank broke down into the water in bays and headlands that endangered the road. Little traffic could have passed along it, for it soon degenerated into a mere cart track, and the tyres refused to grip the slimy weeds of its surface.

Suddenly it broadened out, however, and a pair of brick pillars holding up rusty iron gates appeared upon their left.

They went up a broad drive completely clothed in a green velvet of close-growing moss, and Veronica was at last permitted to stretch her cramped limbs while Lucas banged on a door.

The bell-pull was too firmly rusted home to permit of its ringing, and Lucas, after an assault upon the knocker that echoed like a bombardment through the silent house, leaving Veronica in the company of the motor-bike, went pushing through an overgrown shrubbery in search of the caretaker.

At the end of close upon half an hour Veronica, exhausted, frightened, and filled with a nameless horror by her dank and mouldering surroundings, heard sounds of movement approaching through the silent house; a great rattling of bolts followed, and the opening door revealed Lucas's sharp-cut and somewhat drawn features, with a hag-like face peering over his shoulder.

The leathern racing helmet he wore, backed by the marble pilasters of the porch, made Lucas look exactly like an Egyptian priest, and the huddled figure at his side seemed some strange familiar he had invoked for his magical work.

A dingy crimson dressing-gown had been hastily dragged on over an unbelievably dirty pink flannelette nightgown, for the woman had been aroused from her slumbers by the simple expedient of putting half a brick through her bedroom window.

She peered at Veronica through hanging elf-locks of grey hair and, addressing her as 'dearie', started a long rigmarole, apparently of apology for the state of the house and garden, but so toothless was she, that not one word could be made out.

Lucas solved the problem of this address of welcome by pushing her aside, and taking the now almost fainting girl by the arm, he led her into the house.

'Come along,' he said, 'there is one decent room in this mausoleum, anyway. We will have a fire put in it and the place will soon look more cheerful.'

He led the shrinking girl down a long passage to what had apparently been a billiard room, though the table was gone. Rugs covered the polished floor, low bookcases stood round the walls from the tops of which enormous fish goggled at the intruders in their varnished dignity. Guns stood in a rack at one end, and a litter of fishing tackle filled all four corners.

Lucas dropped Veronica into one of the great leather armchairs and went to open the shutters, letting in a flood of early morning sunshine, and when the hag, who, for all her years, moved with a mouselike quickness, returned with a bundle of brushwood and kindled a fire upon the great open hearth, the place looked far from unprepossessing. An oval mahogany table inlaid according to Victorian taste stood in the window, and Lucas and the hag between them carried it over to the fire. In a marvellously short space of time bacon and eggs and tea appeared upon it, and the two travellers who since their entry into this dismal house had hardly addressed each other, set to work upon their welcome meal.

Nothing but the commonplaces of the table passed between them till Lucas lit his after-breakfast pipe.

'Listen to me, Veronica,' he said. 'That is, if you can keep your eyes open, and you had better keep them open until I have told you what I have to say, because it is very important. We are in a very tight hole, both of us, at the present moment. The trouble may blow over. On the other hand, it may not, and then we shall have to look out for squalls. I shall know pretty soon. All you have to do is to stop here and keep absolutely quiet. You can't talk to this old dame, whatever her name is, because you can't make her hear, and you mustn't try to talk to anyone else. Don't communicate with your friends, either, especially the Ashlotts, this is most important, because your only chance of safety is for no one to know of your existence. Understand this, Veronica, we are in grave danger, very grave danger, both of us.'

Veronica had only to look at his strained face to know that he spoke the truth, or at least what he believed to be the truth, but she did not feel alarmed. Horror she might feel of the house and the whole situation, but she felt no anxiety for her personal safety. Her companion, however, seemed to take a different view of the matter.

Lucas, glancing at his watch every other minute, allowed himself half an hour's rest, and then he announced that he must set out on his return journey. He heaved himself out of his chair and stood looking at Veronica as if he expected some move upon her part. She, however, stared vaguely back at him as usual, not knowing what was expected of her by this unaccountable being.

'Aren't you coming to see me off?' he said.

She rose obediently, and followed him, dog-like as usual, across the tiled hall to the front door. In the porch he paused, and looked steadfastly at the girl beside him. Then he suddenly caught her and drew her to him.

'Veronica,' he said, 'you've got no one to look to but me, and I've got no one but you; we have got to stick together.'

Veronica's soft little heart was easily touched. She only saw the man's face, strained, tired, and anxious, close to hers; everything that had gone before was forgotten, it was a different Lucas, changed and softened, who stood before her now. Almost involuntarily she smiled back at him. It was the first time Lucas had ever seen her smile, and so completely did it change her face that he hardly knew her for the same girl; his arms tightened about her, and before he knew what he was doing, he had kissed her.

Then, reluctantly, he released her and turned away. Half

in the saddle of his cycle, and half out if it, he paused, and looked at Veronica again; then suddenly he leant towards her.

'I shall come back again,' he said. 'I shall come back again, dear, whether or no. Wait for me, Veronica.'

CHAPTER SIX

Sounds in the hall of the big house in the Bloomsbury square showed that the members of the council were assembling for their meeting. The butler, who was also a lay brother, was admitting them, and one by one they passed down the long tiled passage to the room built out at the back, which was designed for a billiard room but was now the lodge of an occult fraternity.

In the office the secretary of that society was gathering together the papers that concerned the business about to be transacted. A close observer might have noticed that the lines of the man's dark face had deepened, adding some ten years to his apparent age, and that his eyes appeared to be deep sunk in his head and heavy-lidded; save for that, and some dust-covered motoring clothes, rolled hastily into a bundle and thrown into the corner there was nothing to show that he had travelled over two hundred miles during the night.

His papers made ready, he paused, and unlocking a cupboard that stood upon the safe, he poured himself out the best part of half a tumblerful of whisky and swallowed down the raw spirit without water. By the time he had walked down the passage that led to the billiard room the lines also had gone from his face.

The members of the council had already assembled, and the secretary's entrance was the signal for them to take their places about the table and proceed to the transaction of business. The minutes of the preceding meeting were read and signed, and the matters on the agenda proceeded as usual; then came the time when the chairman said: 'Any other business?' and looked from face to face of the men surrounding the table. Each responded with a shake of the head, and the man at the foot of the table was permitting his lungs to expand in a sigh of relief when the chairman broke the silence.

'There is a matter, brethren, which I should like to lay before you, and upon which I should value your advice.

'Last night a ritual was being worked in this Lodge, the ritual of the Seventh Degree. I was in the Chair. Suddenly I perceived a figure materialize upon the floor of the lodge, several of the other brethren perceived it also. By means of a Word of Power I was able to banish it, and we proceeded with the ritual, but it is a very serious thing that any *cowan* should have been able to pass through the seal set upon the room.'

Grave faces received this announcement. They knew how serious the matter was. Occult fraternities guarded their secrets, not only physically, but mentally by means of the mystic seals they set upon their meeting places, and here was a fraternity, one of the oldest and most powerful in the western hemisphere, faced by the fact that a stranger had succeeded in penetrating into the working of one of their highest degrees.

The old man with the long white beard upon the chairman's left spoke first.

'Are you sure that it was a *cowan*? I have known it happen that a member of the Fraternity, taken over to the Other Side by sudden death, had attended lodge from sheer habit, forgetting that he was no longer in the body.'

These men were as accustomed to functioning out of the body as in it. There appeared nothing strange in the statement that the dead had returned, they were used to sitting in council with men who had been dead for hundreds of years or who were separated from them by the breadth of a continent. The only thing that puzzled them was, how the seal upon their meeting place had been broken by one who was not entitled to enter, and the chairman replied: 'It could not have been a member of the Fraternity, because it was a woman.'

Lucas waited with suspended breath to learn whether the intruder had been sufficiently clearly materialized to be recognizable; he dared not ask any questions; the pupils of his eyes had contracted to pinpoints and his face was set like a mask.

The discussion turned this way and that for some minutes, and the consensus of opinion seemed to be that some outsider with considerable occult knowledge had succeeded in breaking the seal and effecting an entrance. Such a thing had not happened since the sixteenth century, when the Paris lodge had been similarly invaded, and to this occurrence they turned for a precedent that should guide them in their course of action.

The Fraternity had in its keeping the secret of the use of the Punitive Dark Rays of disintegration, and these it was permitted to employ upon the occasions, happily rare, when its secrets were in danger of being revealed to the uninitiated. Not that the brethren were blood-thirsty men, but the secret knowledge entrusted to them was of such power that its dissemination among those unfit for such a supreme trust was a very serious matter indeed, too serious to be trifled with; and when occult knowledge got into unworthy hands, those who were responsible for its safe custody were required to prevent effectually any use or spread of such knowledge; if a man chose to spy upon their secrets, then he must take the consequences, for the knowledge was not theirs to communicate at will, neither had they the right to pardon a transgression. Some of the brethren, having regard to the fact that the transgressor was believed to be a woman, though the chairman was not absolutely certain upon this point, hesitated to cast their votes in favour of action; and though no one actually refused to sanction the use of the Dark Ray upon this occasion, two abstained from voting, so the remaining five carried the decision.

They had a grave trust to fulfil in safeguarding the knowledge placed in their keeping. Someone had learnt their secrets, and that person must, at all costs, be effectually silenced, only thus could their trust be held to have been fulfilled.

Lucas himself was perfectly safe; the brethren had no means of associating the intruder with himself; she, and she alone would be struck by the Dark Ray. He had only to send round once more to the secretarial agencies of London in order to replace her with a sensitive equally or almost as good. Yet he sat staring at the chairman like a hypnotized man, his soul frozen with horror. Absorbed in their discussion, no one looked at the secretary, or his face must surely have betrayed him. Lucas, who had thought himself beyond good or evil, immune from emotion, had been humanized, and his humanity betrayed him. A man upon the Left-Hand Path finds his strength in separateness; Lucas had formed a tie, he had deviated from his perfect loyalty to evil, the spark of good that was in him had been fanned to a flame, and it was proving his undoing.

The brethren were discussing ways and means, who were to be responsible for the task in hand, and the time and place at which they should meet for the united meditation that should let loose the Dark Ray, and they did not realize that anything untoward was afoot until the scrape of a thrust-back chair drew their attention to the foot of the table.

Lucas was upon his feet; his face was a peculiar grey-white, absolutely bloodless. For a long minute the men round the table stared at him, arrested by the expression of his face. It seemed as if he would never find his voice, and then, with difficulty, the words came.

'There is something I wish to say to you,' he said.

The chairman signed to him to go on. For some time past the secretary had been an object of suspicion, and it did not come as any surprise to the men present that Lucas was

70

involved in the affair under consideration. They waited for him to pull himself together. Presently he spoke again.

'This matter is not quite as you think it is.'

Another long pause followed as Lucas sought for the words that would not come. The men round the table waited immobile in the half-light of the shaded lamp, their gaze directed towards him, no one offering to help him out.

With a renewed effort he continued.

'The person you saw in the lodge was not directly concerned in the matter. She was entirely passive. A trance medium in fact. She is not responsible for anything that has happened.'

'Then,' said the chairman, 'if she is not responsible, who is?'

'I am,' said Lucas. 'I was operating her.'

'In what way?'

'Under hypnosis.'

'Has she any recollection of what has happened?'

'No, none; I swear she hasn't. She was nothing but a tool. She had no more to do with it than a pen with what it signs. If you want to strafe anybody, you can strafe me. I am the person responsible.'

It was a strange scene in that darkened Bloomsbury room. The circle of men round the table, their faces dimly illumined by the reflected light from the shaded lamp; behind them, a shadowy altar with the Everlasting Fire glowing dimly upon it; and before them, erect, tense, solitary, the man who was about to die.

For there could be no doubt as to what the verdict would be. A long time ago the Chiefs had known that Lucas was unsuitable to be a member of the Fraternity. For some time past it had been suspected almost to certainty that he was intriguing against them, and now they had caught him red-handed. He, a member of the outer temple, had obtained possession of the secrets of the inner temple up to the seventh degree; they were not only angry at the theft, but thoroughly alarmed that such a theft had been possible, and their alarm made them ruthless.

The chairman spoke. 'There are two courses open to us should a man obtain the secrets of a degree he is not entitled to. Either we can administer the oath of the degree to him, or – we can silence him. Are you willing that the oath should be administered to our brother here present?'

One by one, as he glanced at them, the men shook their heads. 'Then,' said the chairman, 'we have no option but to proceed with the other course.'

He did not put the vote to the meeting, it was doubtful if he could have got the men to vote, for it was a sentence of death they were passing, and though their minds were made up, to give that deciding nod was not easy, and the motion would have passed without opposition if the voice of the old man with the long white beard had not broken the silence.

'Though we are not willing to admit this man to the degrees he has desecrated, is there no other course than – to invoke the Dark Ray?'

'What other course would you suggest?' replied the chairman.

'Can we not bind him with an oath, and bid him depart?'

'What have the brethren to say upon the matter?' said the chairman, looking round at the assembled men again.

There was a long silence, no one caring to take the responsibility of voicing the thought that was in the minds of all of them. The man they were trying stood tense as a bow-string, his nostrils twitching like an animal's and his eyes, now opaque as marble, now pools of blackness.

At length the journalist broke the silence. 'Daren't risk it. Can't trust him,' he said, and the rest breathed a sigh of relief that they had been spared the voicing of the verdict.

'Is that your opinion?' asked the chairman, again referring to the assembled men, who, each in his way, by a nod or a half-spoken word, assented; save only the patriarch, and his voice once more broke upon the assembly.

'We have long known this man for what he is,' he said.

'A man dedicated to the services of evil, following the Left-Hand Path, a black occultist; and yesterday, had I been asked, I should have voted as you have done. But can we say that this man is wholly given over to evil, to separateness? Remember, you are condemning him upon a voluntary confession. Unless he had spoken, we should never have known, and he has elected to sacrifice himself rather than that an innocent person should suffer.'

'A man in love will do anything,' said the journalist, and Lucas started as if hot metal had touched him. The words, or the sneer with which they were spoken, seemed to galvanize him into activity; for a moment he stood there, as if poised for flight, and then his hand went to his hip pocket, and the assembly found themselves looking down the barrel of a revolver.

'If you want me, you can come and fetch me,' he snarled. 'Strafing is a game that two can play at.' And he backed slowly towards the door, glaring at them along the shining barrel of the revolver.

'You can put up your weapon, Mr Lucas,' said the chairman coldly. 'We shall not use physical force.'

Lucas slammed the door behind him and turned the key. The lodge-room was remote from the house and the Ashlotts' abode in the basement. Some delay must occur before the brethren could escape. He dashed down the long tiled passage to the office, snatched the papers out of his private safe, and raced upstairs to his bedroom. Here he caught up just such personal belongings as might readily be thrust into a haversack; then he rushed downstairs again.

A thundering upon the door at the end of the tiled passage showed that he was only just in time, and catching up a handful of letters that had fallen from the letter-box upon the hall mat, he passed out of the old house in the Bloomsbury square where his life had been lived and his life-work had been done. A new order of existence opened before

73

him; what it held for him was unknown, and never had any man more completely burnt his boats behind him.

Soon he was speeding down the road. The excitement of the happenings buoyed him up and he felt no fatigue, but as he drew clear of the London traffic into the open country roads and had time for thought, a realization of his position dawned upon him. He was out of a job to begin with, and little prospect of getting one. He was not penniless; he had a small sum in the bank, but it would not last the two of them very long. Veronica had nothing but what she stood up in, and he very little more. They could probably 'squat' indefinitely in the general's fishing box, and he might be able to make some use of his pen, but it was a precarious living at best.

Lucas was not an introspective man; if he had been, he might have noticed that his resources would last just twice as long for one as for two. He dared not use Veronica again, and there was no reason why he should not cut loose from her; one is not obliged to employ a secretary one does not require. All the same it never occurred to him to abandon her. For the first time in his life the man's strange nature had formed a tie. He had not yet had time to reason things out, but a flash of self-revelation had come to him at the words of the journalist, 'A man in love will do anything.' Was he in love with Veronica? He hardly even asked himself the question; he only knew that with the instinct of a homing pigeon, he was going back to her as fast as his machine would take him. She was the only creature with whom he was in touch in the midst of an alien and hostile world; bereft of Veronica he would be utterly alone.

The mileage he had travelled began to tell upon him, and it was a very weary man who looked down from the crest of the hills upon the valley of Beckering, spread out in the afternoon sun. By the time he reached the rough cart track along the river bank it was all he could do to hold the cycle steady. Knowing it to be useless to ring the bell, he made his way round through the shrubbery to the rear of the

74

house. Veronica, sitting over her tea, looked up to see him come with uncertain steps across the grass and knock upon the french window for admission. She sprang up to let him in, and he crossed the threshold without a word and dropped into a chair beside the table. She asked no questions, she never did. He was a remote, unaccountable being upon whom she had no claims, but her woman's instinct made her give him a cup of tea and watch with satisfaction while he drank it. His face and clothes were covered with a mask of dust, and he looked more than ever like the statue of some fallen Egyptian king in a forgotten tomb.

There was a curiously changed 'feel' about him; he no longer conveyed a sense of power and aloofness. The mysterious force he always seemed to emanate was gone. He was simply a very tired man, and in some subtle way he had drawn very much closer to her. He drank, but would not eat; and when the third cup of tea had passed his dust-grimed lips he rose stiffly to his feet, and laid a hand upon Veronica's shoulder.

'I'm going to sleep. I'm absolutely done in. Watch by me. Don't leave me alone.' And he flung himself, dust and all, upon a broad leather sofa that stood at the side of the hearth.

He gave her no reason why she should watch beside him while he slept, he would have found it difficult to have formulated one to himself, but he felt the greatest aversion from being left alone.

Veronica watched the golden afternoon light fade to dusk, and then a shuffling in the passage announced the advent of the old caretaker with supper. When she saw Lucas asleep on the sofa, she mumbled something unintelligible and went to fetch a second plate; she seemed quite to have accepted their presence in the house for which she was responsible.

Roused by her movements, Lucas woke up, and arose to go and wash off the dust. As he shed his motoring overalls, he felt something bulky in the pocket, and drew out the bundle of letters he had picked up as he left the house. Two were for the Ashlotts, the rest for the Fraternity, but one was addressed to him personally. The Ashlotts' letters he tore up and flung in the hearth, he dared not risk sending them on, his safety lay largely in the ignorance of the brethren as to his whereabouts, for it is very difficult to focus an occult force unless one has some idea as to at least the point of the compass to which it is to be directed. The letters for the Fraternity he glanced through out of pure curiosity; their writers would have to wait for an answer; then he opened the letter addressed to himself. It was brief and to the point, and without any preamble, informed him that General Sawberry had passed peacefully away at his Woking home early the previous morning, and that he himself was the principal legatee. Lucas let out a long whistle. What astonishing luck, and just when he needed it, too. If the rest of his luck were as good as this, he would pull through all right. He put the letter in his pocket and went down to supper, patting Veronica on the back in the most friendly fashion as he took his seat at the table.

After supper, smoking a pipe, and covertly watching Veronica as she read, he again congratulated himself upon his good fortune. He was master of this house, queer old ramshackle place though it was. He asked nothing better than to be left alone in the possession of his newly acquired resources.

If only the Fraternity *would* let him alone! Perhaps if he disappeared completely from their ken they would forget all about him in time, or at any rate get over their rage. He did not wish to think about that Dark Ray and its effects, they were not a pleasant subject of meditation. He remembered the German-American who had preferred to plunge into Niagara Gorge rather than face exposure to the force of that ray. If it had not been for Veronica, he himself would have followed some such course. But there was Veronica, with the lamplight throwing into relief the soft curves of chin and throat, and who held his attention and interest in

76

a queer, subtle fashion. He longed to win some sort of response from her, just such another smile as she had given him upon his departure for London. He sat there, watching her in that dim-lit, tobacco-clouded room, planning how he might bring that smile to her lips again. The dog-like, cowed Veronica was of no use to him, he wanted a Veronica who would come of her own free will, and, above all, would smile.

He could not forget that smile; it was the first time any woman had shown him that side of her nature; the first time, indeed, that he had ever sought to call it forth. Those smiles are not bestowed upon cynical, cold-blooded men, such as he had trained himself to be. But fundamentally Lucas was neither cynical nor cold-blooded, he was a hot-blooded man with quick emotions and strong enthusiasms. He had always believed that the race can best be served by those who have no tie or bond of affection, forgetting that a man who has never loved does not know how to love.

And now Lucas was getting a new training. As he had surmised, he and Veronica had followed the Way of Initiation together for many lives until he had quitted the Path, and then their ways had divided. But now, with her re-entry upon the scene of his life, the old influence was reasserting itself and he was being slowly drawn back towards the Path.

His loyalty to Veronica had been prompted by a dread of losing her rather than any concern for her welfare, but still, it was love, a germinating seed, if not the perfect flower.

CHAPTER SEVEN

Next morning Lucas, accompanied by Veronica, set out to explore his little estate. With the exception of the lawn in front of the house, the rest of the grounds consisted of shrubbery and woodland, both much overcrowded and neglected. Straggling laurels grew up like small trees, and oaks, herded together in ragged negligence, lost all their native dignity and contrived to produce a sinister twilight in the underworld of their groves. Lucas had no intention of reconstructing this domain, but it pleased him to explore its resources.

Only the cart track lay between the grounds and the river, and as the boundary was marked by a single strand of slack and rusting wire, the division was more legal than actual. Many trees had fallen and lay slowly rotting in the green twilight on the shadowed river, for here the bed deepened and the banks narrowed, and the current ran through a gorge of overhanging trees. Occasionally a vole plopped into the water; occasionally a kingfisher shot like a streak of blue down the narrow path of sunlight in the river's centre, and Lucas spoke of life in general, and his own in particular.

Veronica, though she was no talker, was an admirable listener, for she had a quick and receptive mind, able to grasp the significance of new ideas. She considered and stored away for future reference the concepts of men and things that were being presented to her. For the first time she heard the doctrine of the immortality of the soul brought to its logical conclusion as Lucas talked glibly of past lives and their influence upon the present, treating these subjects with an easy familiarity which showed that they were part of the habitual content of his consciousness. To him, death was on a par with emigration, a serious undertaking for a poor man, but merely an interesting and exciting adventure for the man rich in knowledge. Premature death, however, he objected to strongly, not because he feared to die, but because of the time it took to train a new body for service.

Veronica found herself brought face to face with a new set of values in life; the body, the world, held cheap and made to serve an end of which no hint had hitherto reached her; indeed, Lucas did not even speak of 'the body', but of 'a body', and the world was regarded as a world of effects, with but little power to set up causes on its own account. What happened there was to Lucas an aftermath, the real struggle, the real event, had taken place upon a subtler plane; Veronica found the concept presented to her of great forces, governed by great laws, that operated behind the multiplex happenings of our haphazard existence; the aim of Lucas's life she learnt, was to discover the nature of these laws and so control their forces by balancing one against the other that the power of his will, infinitesimal though it was by comparison, should be able to turn the scale.

Now Veronica, though she neither talked nor reasoned, was not a fool. She soon perceived that, while Lucas talked much of the occult powers and the means of their attainment, he gave no hint as to the use he meant to make of them when once attained. She set herself to work, in her quiet little way, to find out what his ultimate aim might be, and she speedily discovered that he had not got one. He was playing with these powers as a child might play with a Meccano outfit, making little models that would hoist little weights, all designed upon the best engineering principles, but with never a thought of the greater purposes of life to which these principles might be applied. He studied the Secret Science for the delight of seeing the parts fit together and the mystery explained; and that great study, which is as much a religion as a science, was no more to him than a jigsaw puzzle.

Lucas, absorbed in his narrative, never heeded his listener's attitude, till, pausing to search for a word, he found himself being surveyed with a quaint detachment and experienced an unpleasant feeling that in some way or other he had been making a fool of himself. Anxious to ascertain her attitude, he shot a question at her, for the first time that morning.

'Well? What do you make of it all?'

Veronica nodded her head sagely. 'I think I see what you mean; there are things that cause other things to happen, and you want to know what they are so that you can get at them.'

That's about it,' said Lucas. 'The control of causation, if you want to be precise.'

'But what are you going to do with them when you have got hold of them?'

'You can do anything you like with them, you could get anything you wanted.'

'But one doesn't want such an awful lot.'

'Come now, wouldn't you like to have great resources at your disposal?'

'I'd like a certain amount,' said cautious Veronica, 'but not too much; it would take such a lot of looking after. Besides, supposing you were balancing the forces and one of them slipped?'

'That is just exactly what has happened,' muttered Lucas to himself, and fell silent for several minutes. Then he threw off his dark mood and spoke again. 'What would you do with the resources of the world if you had them?'

'I should get some frocks and books and pictures, and a dog; oh yes, I should certainly get a dog.'

'But that would not exhaust the resources of the world;

what would you do with the rest?'

Veronica thought a moment. 'I couldn't eat all the bread in the world, but I could see that the people who needed it got some, and that the greedy people did not gobble too much, which is what they do at present. Why did you never think of doing that, Mr Lucas?'

'Oh, I don't know. What has it got to do with me?'

'But could you be happy, knowing that someone else was starving?'

'Good Lord, yes; that is their look-out. People have got to stand on their own feet; you would never get anywhere if you always waited for the stragglers. Civilization is built upon sacrifice, and if I have any choice in the matter, I propose to be one of the civilized, not one of the sacrificed.'

This was logic hard to answer, and Veronica did not attempt the task. She merely shook her head and said: 'All the same, I don't believe you really like it. You are always after something, and as soon as you get it you want the next thing. It is like the Mad Hatter's tea party – jam yesterday, and jam tomorrow, but never jam today. I like to enjoy myself as I go along.'

Lucas was enjoying himself vastly. Veronica was beginning to wake up, and it thoroughly amused him to reveal unexpected depths to her and listen to her shrewd little comments. There was more in her than he had expected; her mind was not empty so much from lack of capacity as from lack of raw material. He imagined that he was doing a very great deal to Veronica; he little realized how much Veronica was doing to him. He, as well as she, was being presented with a new view point; he might sweep aside her naïve little assertions, but he could not ignore the fact that, quaintly though they might be expressed, they were singularly relevant, and that she had an uncanny knack of putting her finger on the weak spots in his position. Perhaps there was something to be said for her point of view after all; he himself had already experienced a keener enjoyment than he had ever known before in getting into sympathetic touch with this child; it was quite a different sensation to that of power. The manipulation of another being had its charms, of course, but they palled when the novelty wore off; but when, instead of manipulating, and controlling, one could win another person to respond, why, then one was, in turn, stimulated, lifted on to a higher level. It opened up new vistas, new possibilities of experience, this action and reaction of two, as opposed to the solitary working of the one. But to achieve this interaction, one had to win the other to a willing co-operation.

He knew exactly how he meant to work upon her mind, how to rouse her nature so that she should expand from the child into the woman and make that response. He was already well acquainted with her character – or thought he was – and he knew just how he meant to touch those secret springs that let loose the forces which lie latent in the natures of even the quietest.

The old caretaker had prepared supper and Veronica had seated herself at table when he made his belated entry. The meal was quite a festive occasion; Lucas absorbed in his new pursuit was in an especially cheerful mood, and Veronica, who was fast losing her fear of him, was quite prepared to respond.

But to some extent it was she who was pulling the strings of *his* nature, not he of hers; it was the deep fountains of *his* being that were unsealed, while she, aloof as only those who are of virgin soul can be aloof, looked on, half frightened, half fascinated, at the forces she had roused, but, being a woman, thoroughly enjoying herself. He had always had a queer kind of fascination for her, and the fascination, in some curious way, was enhanced by the fact that she was afraid of him, so that, before the meal had ended, Veronica was drawn once again to smile upon Lucas.

And the smile completed his undoing. It dawned slowly, like the smile of Mona Lisa, glowed for a moment with a revelation of all that could be in a woman, and then fled suddenly, as if alarmed at its own temerity. Lucas had set out to play a game, but he found himself caught in a current of the greater deeps. Men have thrown away kingdoms for just such a smile, and Lucas threw away his soul. His only chance of safety in the present crisis lay in allegiance to his Dark Master whose law is separateness; only thus could he draw upon the force necessary to withstand the attack that was arrayed against him.

Separateness might mean power, but it was in union that happiness lay, and union could only come through love, and now that Lucas had tasted love, he desired nothing else.

The moon was up by the time the meal was finished, for meals go slowly under such circumstances. The clear cold radiance shone white upon the lawn save where the shadows of the shrubbery fell black as ink. The summer night in that shut-in valley was almost as warm as the day, and they went out through the french windows on to the terrace. There, as they strolled up and down, Lucas slipped his hand through Veronica's arm; the long, olive-brown fingers in sharp contrast to the girl's white skin; and she, half child, half woman, was well content to let it rest there.

So they strolled and turned, and strolled and turned, talking of life as each had seen it. She heard how Lucas had been born outside wedlock, the son of a man who stood high in political circles; how he had been brought up in the family of a small shopkeeper, and how the family circle had failed to contain him. A square peg had been driven into a round hole, but it was the hole that had split under the pressure. Then came the history of a rebellious, unmanageable lad, who jumped in and out of jobs as the hot southern temperament of his mother flared up within him; but presently the intellect of his father began to assert itself, and he struggled in night school to supplement the grammar school education that had been prematurely terminated by his irruption into freedom.

At length he found himself as assistant to an old man who kept a second-hand shop. Into this abode of unhallowed dust came one day a curious article. It was a white, or rather Isabella-coloured dust-sheet some three yards square, upon which a circle, four feet in diameter had been drawn. The interior of the circle was left blank, but around its circumference was a most extraordinary collection of strange hieroglyphs and rude representations of creatures and things. The owner of the shop accepted the thing at its face value; a dust sheet was a dust sheet to him, and could be used for covering up the stock.

The active-minded lad, however, was not so easily satisfied. Every time he unfurled the thing at night, he would puzzle over its hieroglyphs, and every time he bundled it up in the morning he would renew his quest. Then, one day when business was slack, he was looking through some of the books that lay about the shop and in one of them he found the clue to the mystery in a rough wood-cut of which the dust sheet was evidently a copy. Wild with excitement he learned that the mysterious sheet was a floor-cloth used by a magician when he wished to invoke certain elemental presences. The operator stood in the centre of the magic circle, and protected by the symbols that surrounded him, called upon the beings of another order of creation to take their stand each on his own sigil depicted upon the corners of the cloth.

When closing-time came the young assistant locked the door from the inside, and spreading the magic dust-sheet took his stand in the centre of the circle and read aloud to the shadows the magical formula which the book declared to be suitable to the occasion. Then he waited.

Absolutely nothing happened, and disgusted with the whole proceeding he went home, and to bed. As he was dozing off to sleep, however, he was aroused to consciousness by the feeling that there was something in the room. He tried to reach out his hand to strike a light, but found himself powerless to move. He felt a breath in his face, a weight on his chest. Something was at his throat, and still he could not move. Then, with a supreme effort of will he sat up, but found the room empty, even as the shop had been.

Being a lad of sound nerves, he soon settled down and went to sleep again, and would have thought no more of his nightmare had it not been that in the morning he perceived that the floor was covered with slimy tracks as if an army of slugs had passed across it. The foul trail led from the window to the bed and back again, and when he examined it, he found that the window frame was covered with the filthy stuff. The creature that had left the trail had evidently entered by the six-inch aperture left open at the top of the window for ventilation.

For many nights after that the boy slept with his window shut, but the miscellaneous collection of books that had come, along with the floor-cloth, from the house of some student of the occult arts, so inflamed his imagination that he could think of nothing else. His whole soul was gathered up into a one-pointed desire to learn the secret of the mystery to which he had been given a clue. What was it men sought by these mysterious means? How did they seek it, and who were the seekers?

One evening, as he was spreading the magic dust-sheet over the more precious of the rubbish, he saw a face peering at him through the window, and in a minute or two the owner of the face appeared in the doorway, and an individual of uncouth and hairy appearance demanded the price of the dust-sheet. Lucas named a figure and without demur the stranger paid. Then he peered curiously at the lad.

'Do you know anything about these things?' he inquired.

Lucas, like most people in a hostile environment, was exceedingly reserved, but something about the stranger drew while it repulsed him, and before he knew what he was doing, he had embarked upon the story of his invocation and the subsequent slug-tracks. The stranger

85

fairly danced with glee, and almost without his consent, Lucas, the book, and the floor-cloth were hailed round to the stranger's lodgings. There, huddled together inside the protecting circle, Lucas and the stranger read out the invocation in unison. So far as Lucas could see, nothing whatever happened, but the stranger, squinting horribly, announced that the Powers invoked had duly appeared in their appointed places, and thereupon embarked upon an elaborate, arm-waving incantation, for it seems it was one thing to call them up, and quite another to get rid of them. However, after some minutes of droning and manoeuvring, the stranger pronounced the room clear of the Presences, and they sat down to a supper of sausages.

That was the first of many suppers. Lucas never overcame his repulsion for the man, but his studies fascinated him, and he would return night after night to hear his host discourse of Paracelsus, Roger Bacon, Robert Fludd, and the knowledge that had died with them. There was a miscellaneous collection of books in the frowsy lodgings, and the keen-minded lad soon had gathered the gist of them and drawn his own conclusions. A very little experimenting sufficed to show him that there was something tangible lying behind all the verbiage, but he also saw that the heart of the matter was not set down in the books. If he wanted knowledge he would have to find someone who had that knowledge. As he was raking in the bins of a second-hand book shop one evening, he fell into conversation with a man engaged in the same occupation.

His new acquaintance was a very different type of man to the purchaser of the floor-cloth. He was, in fact, none other than the old man with the white beard who always sat upon the chairman's left at the meetings of the council. Taking the measure of the shabby lad, he had decided that here was a mind of no ordinary calibre, and had taken him under his wing; books were at the boy's disposal, and the stimulus of the conversation of a scholar had any stimulus been needed, and for the first time in his life, Lucas found himself in a congenial atmosphere. It was not long before initiation into the outer temple of the Fraternity followed, and Lucas found that that which he had so long sought was his, for good or evil.

Passed on from one introduction to another, Lucas made his way into Fleet Street and rose rapidly until his journalistic career was cut short by his appointment to the secretaryship of the Fraternity.

Then began the struggle between the idealism of the brethren and the fierce ambition of the man who was among them but not of them. Lucas told the story in vivid detail, never sparing himself, but using Veronica as a confessional for the relief of that which so long had been pent up within him without any means of expression.

Before the story drew to its close the moon had set, and darkness and dewfall drove them to take refuge in the house. Upon the step of the french windows they paused, reluctant to leave the cool night for the close stuffiness of a lamp-lit room.

Veronica lifted her hand. 'Listen,' she said, 'foxhounds.'

'Nonsense,' said Lucas. 'They don't hunt at this time of year, or at this time of night, either, for that matter.'

'But listen,' cried the girl, 'they are quite close; listen to the way they are baying.'

To her ears the bell-like notes of hounds hunting in view were coming nearer and nearer through the woods; then she suddenly clutched her companion's arm.

'Mr Lucas,' she cried, 'they are not on the ground, they are overhead, in the air!'

She felt herself suddenly snatched through the window and the shutters slammed behind her. Lucas, ghastly-faced, stared at her for a moment without speaking, and then dropped into a chair by the table and buried his face in his arms.

Veronica, poor child, gazed at him, helpless and distressed. The belling of the hounds that seemed to come from high overhead in the darkness sounded incredibly sinister, and the sight of the man bowed in distress over the table filled her with fear and foreboding even while it made her heart ache in sympathy for his uncomprehended trouble.

She laid a timid hand on his shoulder. 'What is it? What is the matter?'

For answer an arm reached out and encircled her and drew her to him, and he hid his face in the folds of her dress. For a long while they remained thus, the man rigid and motionless, the girl with her hand resting on his shoulder, every now and again stroking the rough tweed of his coat to convey the comfort she knew not how to express.

Finally, he raised his face, curiously changed, and looked at her.

'Those were the astral hunting-dogs,' he said. 'The Hounds of Heaven. They hunt traitors with them.'

'Who hunt traitors?' said Veronica.

'The brethren. And it was I who taught them to do it, too. And now they are hunting me. They didn't like the new spirit in the Fraternity, but they make use of it all right when it suits them.'

'But they can't be hunting you with dogs!'

'No, they don't hunt with the dogs, they only use them to locate me; it is the Ray they will use to kill me.'

'Oh, but it isn't possible, it is all a bad dream.'

'It is no dream, Veronica. They mean to kill me, and they are quite right. I am better dead, and if it were not for you, I should be glad to go, but I do not want to go now I have known you.'

He rose to his feet and faced her, the pupils of his eyes narrowed to pinpoints, his expression very evil, as she had not seen it for many days past.

'But I am not going,' he said. 'Not very far, at any rate.'

He felt in his pocket and produced a pen-knife and opened it, and, before she realized what he was about, drove the blade into her arm.

'Don't be frightened,' he said, as with a cry of mingled pain and terror she strove to escape from him. 'I won't hurt you. I am only doing this in order that I may be able to keep in touch with you when I get over on the other side. It is the blood-link that savages use when they admit a stranger to the tribe, and it holds even through death. It is stronger than marriage.' Then, holding her in a grip she could not resist, he raised the bleeding arm to his mouth and sucked the blood.

She gazed at him in horror mingled with amazement. This was the old Lucas back again, the Lucas she had almost forgotten. He let go her arm, but retained his grip on her wrist so that she could not run away.

'Don't be angry with me,' he said. 'I did not hurt you much, did I?' Then he put both hands on her shoulders and looked straight into her eyes. 'Listen, Veronica, I may have to go, but I shall not go far. I shall come back again, keep a look-out for me.'

She still looked at him speechlessly, the old mute terror beginning to rise in her eyes. He drew her to him, and laid his cheek against hers. 'Be nice to me, Veronica. I may have to go soon.'

The tone of the man's voice, the ominous stillness of the silent house overcame Veronica, and she burst into tears and clung to him sobbing. For a while they stood thus, and then he gently released himself. 'That is midnight striking, I must go. The Lodge sits at midnight. Kiss me good night, Veronica.'

Of her own free will she flung her arms round his neck and kissed him.

CHAPTER EIGHT

Veronica's sleep was troubled by dreams of foreboding. Through her dreams wandered the figure of Lucas, sometimes as the man she had known when she first went to live in the house in the Bloomsbury square, and at other times as the man who had talked to her in the wood beside the river, opening up wide vistas of life that passed far beyond her horizon, and yet tempting her to go on and on as the white road tempts the traveller. But chiefly did he seem to her to be in some strange unfathomable need that he could not explain, appealing to her for a help whose nature she could not divine. He would appear suddenly in the mazes of her dreams, holding out hands of entreaty, his eyes pools of blackness as they always were when the softer side of his nature was aroused. She would strive towards him, but he always eluded her, and she would toil across vast spaces, knowing him to be in trouble, knowing him to need her, and yet unable to find him. Out of this troubled sleep she would awake every hour, only to find the shadow of impending tragedy awaiting her upon the threshold of consciousness.

Just before dawn, however, a change occurred; the shadow that had been vague, though portentous, suddenly gathered itself together into a definite shape. It condensed, narrowed, lengthened into the form of a great cross-handled sword; for a moment it drew back, as if to gain room for a blow, then it was thrust rapidly outward and downward with the force of some cosmic Arm behind it. For a second it quivered, as if in the heart of a living creature, and then it was withdrawn, and Veronica, falling into a dead sleep, knew no more.

She slept a heavy, dreamless sleep and would probably have slept till noon if she had not been aroused by the old caretaker shaking her violently by the arm. The horrified expression of the old woman's face told her that something had happened, though her toothless mumblings were unintelligible. Wrapping a kimono about her, she followed the old woman to Lucas's room.

He lay upon the bed, stretched straight out, flat upon his back, feet together and arms crossed upon his breast, left over right, like a sculptured figure upon a tomb. The sunlight fell upon his face, and a drift of scarlet petals from the rambler that grew over the window had blown in and lay upon the white bedspread. The bedclothes were untossed, and the pillow bore the single hollow where the dark head rested. The room was utterly and completely still, and Veronica knew that she was alone in it. As quietly and deliberately as a man takes off his clothes, Lucas had withdrawn from his body during the night and passed into the realm of shadows. Whether he had awaited the thrust of the sword, or whether he had unlatched the door and stepped forth, she did not know, all she knew was that this was not death as she had been taught to conceive it. Lucas had gone, leaving his body behind, the olive-skinned body which had served them as a meeting place would be used no more. Whether he would communicate with her again was uncertain, but her friend had not ceased to be. She had no sense of grief or loss, but only of perplexity; how would Lucas manage to re-establish contact with her? Would he remember her, or would he forget? There was no sense of tumult in the room. With his departure the sounds of battle had died away, and now only the peace of emptiness brooded over the room.

She seated herself in a chair beside the window, and gazed out into the sunlit garden, and sometimes at the sunlit face upon the bed.

Presently her solitude was interrupted. A man stood in the doorway surveying the room, in his hand the little brown bag of his calling, a doctor whom the old woman had apparently summoned. He looked from the face on the pillow, stilled by the peace of death, to the face of the woman by the window, who seemed to share equally in the peace. Then he stepped over to the bed and commenced to make his examination without speaking.

'I do not wish him touched,' she said, speaking for the first time that day.

The newcomer replied gently: 'I am afraid he must be touched. There are many things we shall have to do, but you may be quite sure we shall do the very best we can for him, and for you, too. Tell me, are you any relation of his?'

'I am his secretary,' said Veronica.

'Oh,' said the doctor. 'Well, anyway, we will do the best we can for you. But do you know where his relations may be found?'

'No,' said Veronica. 'I do not think he has any.'

'You have not been here many days, have you? Where were you before you came here?' Veronica told him.

'And what were you doing there?'

For one instant, Veronica was about to tell him, and then she knew that she could not. So she fell back upon bald statements of facts. She was in Lucas's employment. He had left his own employment and come down here, bringing her with him. She did not know why he had left his employment. She did not know who his employers were, some sort of a learned society, she thought; at any rate, if the doctor wrote to the Bloomsbury house they would probably give an account of themselves. It was no business of hers, she was well paid, and asked no questions. No, she was no relation of Mr Lucas's, she had already told him so once. No, she did not know what his Christian name was. No, nor his age. He signed documents J. Lucas. No, she did

92

not know what the J stood for, it might be James or it might be John, she had no idea, it was no business of hers, she had never troubled her head about it. She had always addressed him as Mr Lucas. No, she could throw no light on the cause of his death, he had been quite well the night before. He had never complained of any illness, though he had spoken recently of feeling tired. The doctor grasped at this statement as the first tangible thing that had been offered him, and Veronica, as he did not ask, did not feel it incumbent upon her to inform him as to the cause of Lucas's exhaustion; those who deal with the hidden side of things stand apart from their race, and they settle their differences among themselves by their own methods. Veronica did not look upon Lucas as murdered; she knew that he had been forced to abandon his body, but she was quite confident of his ability to look after himself, and pending instructions from him, she would take no action. Finally the doctor coaxed her out of the room and handed her over to the caretaker, who, poor old soul, fussed round her, striving to express her sympathy by inarticulate mumblings.

The long afternoon hours passed slowly, leaving the girl in a half-dreamy state. The next move she could not conjecture, but the game was most certainly not ended, and she had a sense of expectancy, of waiting for something to happen.

The inquest was reported at length in the local papers. The doctor certified that death was due to heart failure brought on by over-exertion; that was all he could say. The most rigorous cross-examination of Veronica, the most careful analysis of the viscera, had failed to reveal any reason why the man should die, he had simply ceased to live, and that was all there was to it. All the same, there was left upon the minds of all who contacted the case the same curious impression, they all felt that there was much that had not been revealed.

They all knew that the young girl who had been the dead man's companion knew more than she chose to tell. They also knew that the hard-faced man who elected to come down from London and who said he was the dead man's employer, was not taking the court into his confidence; and when it transpired that he had in his possession a recently-made will, in which everything was left to the aforesaid young girl, the mystery deepened. It was a riddle to which they could find no solution, so they gave it up, and a verdict was returned of death from natural causes.

After the close of the inquest the hard-faced man came to see Veronica. She was on the terrace when she heard his footsteps on the gravel. He sat himself upon the stone balustrade, leant forward, resting his elbows on his knees, hands clasped, and looked straight into Veronica's eyes, his face close to hers.

'Now, Miss Mainwaring, I want the truth. What is the nature of your association with Lucas?'

'I was his secretary,' replied Veronica.

The man's eyes changed. He looked straight through Veronica, not at her, the eyes out of focus and glazed.

'You are a psychic, and accustomed to leave your body. Tell me, can you go out at will, or has someone got to hypnotize you and push you out?'

'I don't understand what you mean,' said Veronica, looking as blank as she knew how.

'It doesn't matter whether you understand or not. The images rise in your mind, and I can read them. As a matter of fact, you know what I mean perfectly well. Come, Miss Mainwaring, won't you take me into your confidence? I come as a friend, not an enemy; we are quite aware that you were not responsible for the use that was made of your faculties.'

Veronica still elected to look blank, and the man said sharply: 'It is no use pretending that you know nothing, because Lucas confessed the whole business. Moreover, it

94

was I who saw you materialize that night in the Lodge, and as soon as you entered the witness-box I recognized you.'

At this statement, Veronica produced a handkerchief and took refuge in tears. The stern-faced man tugged angrily at his moustache; a woman scores heavily on these occasions.

'It is apparently no use trying to reason with you,' he said, 'but remember this, however much or however little you know, you are not to talk about it. You have seen what happened to one traitor, take care it doesn't happen to another.'

Veronica raised her face from her handkerchief and looked straight at him. During the last few days a new spirit had begun to dawn in her, and it was with that spirit she spoke.

'You take too much upon yourself,' she said. 'You have no right to take the law into your own hands. That was not an execution, it was a murder, and you will have to answer for it. If you had given him time, he would have straightened himself out, but you did not give him time, and now he is dead.'

'That is precisely my own opinion,' said a voice behind them, and they both turned in surprise to find that an old man with a long white beard had crossed the lawn unperceived during their conversation.

'I was responsible for that boy. It was I who put into his hands the knife with which he cut himself, and you should have left him to me to deal with. I could always manage him, he was fond of me in his way, and she and I –' indicating Veronica, with a wave of his corded old hand, 'could have pulled him through between us. Now you have set going causes that we cannot easily calculate. But what is the attitude of this young lady towards the matter?'

'Mulish,' said the hard-faced man, tugging his moustache more furiously than ever. 'I wash my hands of the whole affair.'

'It is a pity that you did not do so sooner,' replied the newcomer coldly, and the hard-faced man turned on his

95

heel and strode off down the path, still tugging his moustache.

'Now, my child,' said the old man, turning to Veronica. 'Let us talk this matter over and see what we can make of it. We know practically everything, so you need not feel that you are giving us information Mr Lucas would not wish us to have. All that we do not know is the nature of your own position in the affair. Did you know what you were doing, or were you a passive tool in his hands?'

'I will tell you nothing,' replied Veronica. 'I don't see why I should answer your questions. You killed Mr Lucas, and you can kill me too, if you want to, but I will tell you nothing about him.'

The old man sighed. 'I cannot urge you further, in the face of the debt you owe him,' he said.

Veronica looked up quickly, in astonishment.

'What debt? What do you mean?'

'Then he has not told you? He did not take you into his confidence?'

'He told me practically nothing. I am in the dark, save for what I have guessed.'

'Then why are you so loyal to him if you are not his partner? You must be his victim, his tool, used more unscrupulously than any man in my experience has ever used a living creature.'

Veronica looked out into the last of the sunset. 'You wouldn't understand if I told you,' she said at length. 'I am not sure if I understand myself, but there was some tie between us. I didn't know its nature, but I was conscious of it. Besides, there is no one to stand by him if I do not, and if no one stands by him, then he will be lost altogether. I think there was something good in him, and I think he would have got better if they had given him a chance.'

The old man held out his hand. 'Go on believing in him,' he said. 'If there is anything that can save him, it is your faith that will do it.' Veronica noticed that he too looked upon Lucas as a living entity, and was about to frame a

96

question, but checked herself lest she should be betraying information the significance of which she could not gauge.

He had retreated a few paces down the path when he returned again. 'He was a much worse man than a child like you can realize,' he said. 'You will want all the faith of which you are capable if you are to regenerate him, and I am going to tell you something in order to reinforce your faith, though I am afraid that it will pain you very much. Do you know that Lucas died in your place.'

Veronica stared at him wide-eyed.

'It was known to the Fraternity of which I am a member that our secrets had been penetrated by some person, and we decided to strike that person, as we are able to do, even though he be unknown to us; and Lucas, knowing this, stood up and said, "That person is nothing but a tool, it is I who am responsible," so the brethren left you alone and struck at him, and I think that they erred grievously in so doing, for they should have known that a man who made that confession had set his face towards the light, and they should have given him time to tread his path.

'My dear, I am afraid you have seen the darker side of the Secret Wisdom; you have seen it used for evil, and you have seen it used in judgement without the saving grace of mercy. But I would ask you to remember this, though perhaps you know it already from your own inner consciousness, for I think you are not wholly asleep to such things, that the power which lies behind the brethren is beneficent. Men may take its name in vain and use it in error; for it is only men of calibre who can carry that force and not be bent and twisted. Therefore do not judge a man harshly who fails in occult work. Do not be misled by our errors, our lack of vision, or the fear that makes men cruel; we serve a reality, my child, though we may not always perceive it clearly.'

Veronica rose and held out her hand to him. 'I am a stranger to you,' she said, 'but I feel that I can trust you. I have no one I can turn to, and there are all sorts of business matters that I do not understand.'

The old man took her hand. 'I accept the responsibility. I pray that I may discharge it better than I did my responsibility towards Lucas.'

The old man stopped with Veronica three days and straightened out her affairs. Not that they were in any great tangle, for Lucas had evidently expected his death and made full preparation for it. The death of General Sawberry some five days before himself had placed him, and consequently Veronica, in possession of a considerable estate, of which the house in the river valley formed an outlying portion. Many affairs had to be settled before Veronica could enter upon the possession of her fortune, and the old man was very anxious for her to leave the gloomy and unhealthy house that had been the scene of the tragedy and make her home with himself and his sister pending the settlement of her affairs. But she refused. She had a feeling that Lucas was not far from her in this place, but that if she left it he would lose track of her, and sinister though he had been in life, and ill-omened though the house might be, yet she could not bring herself to leave it.

Therefore she bade the old man farewell, promising to call upon him if need should arise, and settled down to her solitude with the old caretaker as her sole attendant. No one came near her. The doctor, suspicious of the whole affair, was only too thankful to be clear of it; and the vicar, believing Veronica to be a black sheep, had no mind to prejudice himself in the eyes of his white and woolly flock by trying to save her.

So the days went past. Veronica kept close to the routine that they had followed during the few short hours that she and Lucas had spent there together. In the morning she walked about the grounds and sat upon the log by the river, and in the evening she walked upon the terrace. Between whiles she sat, sometimes in the living-room, and sometimes in the room in which Lucas had died. She believed that in the places which were familiar to him Lucas would wander, and that sooner or later they would meet; but as day followed day and she got no hint of his presence, a chill fear crept into her heart. Was he indeed dead? Dead in the sense in which most people use that word? She knew quite well that he had discarded his physical body but she firmly believed that Lucas as a personality continued to exist – that the organized system of thoughts and feelings that made up his character was still held together by a centralized consciousness, was still actuated by desires and controlled by a purposive will, and it was this organized consciousness that had been her companion, not the five foot nine of flesh and bone that now mouldered in the churchyard.

The summer had changed into autumn, and coming down one day after a night of rain, Veronica found a chill wind blowing. It was too cold to walk in the garden unprotected, so she took from its peg the old trench coat in which Lucas had wrapped her when he brought her down from London, and clad in this garment, she went out into the woods.

Clothes are strange things, they seem to absorb something of the personality of their wearers. Veronica found herself enveloped in the mental atmosphere that Lucas always emanated, and it suddenly seemed to her that he wished her presence by his grave. She had never gone there, for she dreaded the curious eyes of the village. But now, just as she was, hatless, and wrapped in the old trench coat, she set out upon her errand.

By a detour, she reached the church through the woods and entered the burial ground unseen. Two men were engaged in digging a grave, a small grave for a child, and beyond lay three other little mounds. Veronica thought it strange that so many children should have died in so small a village. She kept some bushes between herself and the grave-diggers, but as she passed, a snatch of conversation reached her ears.

'– an' it was four days to the inquest, an' then they adjourned for a week to hear what the doctors in Lunnon had to say, and then Sampson had to coffin him, but Joe Wellan, wot helped, told me that he was as fresh as the day he died, not a mark on him –'

As Veronica passed round the church in search of Lucas's grave, a hand touched her elbow, and she turned to confront a pleasant-faced, fresh-coloured young man who addressed her, hat in hand.

'I – I beg your pardon, but – Miss Mainwaring, is it not?'

Veronica bowed.

'Then, if you will allow me – this is the way,' and he led her through the shrubs to a remote corner of the graveyard, for the instincts of the village men had told them that Lucas was not of their kind, and even in death they had removed him as far as possible from the place where they and their children should lie.

Veronica stood looking down at the mound of rough, newly-turned earth. There lay all that was left of Lucas as the world knew him, and she felt a cold tide of fear rising in her heart. Confronted by this mound of clay among the yew-trees, death, as the world knew death, seemed incontrovertible. The wind blew coldly through the dreary evergreens. She drew the heavy coat she wore closer about her and pulled her feet out of the sodden ground into which they had sunk. A dozen yards away the man who had shown her the grave was still waiting, bare-headed, watching her, and as she turned away from the grave he approached her with an awkward sympathy made still more awkward by the ambiguity of her position. Whatever her relations with Lucas might have been (and the village was quite certain upon this point), he was touched by the sight of the lonely girl coming down to the still lonelier grave.

'I – I'm afraid it is rather rotten for you up at the

Grange,' he began diffidently, 'especially after the shock you have had. It's a nasty place at the best of times.'

Veronica looked up at him steadily for a moment without replying. He was a big-boned, fresh-complexioned young fellow. 'It is very kind of you,' she said, 'but I have not been lonely. After all the trouble was over I was glad to be quiet.'

'But it is a rotten place for a girl up at that Grange. How long are you going to stop there?'

'I don't know,' said Veronica. An hour ago she would have answered that she was going to stop there for the rest of her life, but Lucas was dead, it was all over; there was no point in remaining.

'Are you going back to the Grange now? I can show you a short cut through the woods if you like, it will save you going through the village,' and he led Veronica down a path that passed through a gap in the low stone wall that surrounded the churchyard. 'My name is Alex Butler,' he continued. 'My father is the doctor here.'

'I remember him,' said Veronica. 'He came when Mr Lucas died.'

'Er – yes,' said Alec, awkwardly. 'I say, look at your hand!' he exclaimed. 'It's bleeding.'

Veronica raised her hand in astonishment. A thin line of blood ran down the wrist and a heavy drop fell from her finger-tip upon the dead leaves at her feet. A similar crimson stain marked the grey stones that lay about the ruined wall. Veronica thrust back the stiff sleeve of the trench-coat and found that, drop by drop, blood was welling from the veins of the fore-arm; the wound that Lucas had given her in that strange scene that had been enacted the night of his death, had, for some unknown reason, re-opened, and was bleeding afresh.

'That's quite a gash,' said Butler. 'How did you manage to do it?' and producing a large white handkerchief, he bound it up, not unskilfully. He was in no hurry to complete his task, however, and Veronica suspected that, with a very little encouragement, he would take his ministrations a stage further. She resolutely pulled down the rough sleeve and thrust the injured arm into the breast of her coat. For a moment they stood, however, the man looking down and the girl looking up. They were sheltered from the wind by a hollow, and though it threshed among the tree-tops, the undergrowth was unstirred. But as they stood, a little wandering wind came and blew round them; little vortices of air drew the dead leaves up into miniature whirlwinds, and this wandering draught was cold with a strange cold-ness, like the wind from a cavern. Veronica shivered and drew her coat closer, and Butler, moved by he knew not what impulse, glanced over his shoulder, and simultane-ously they set off down the path at a quickened pace.

Butler accompanied Veronica as far as the strand of slack wire that flanked the rusting gates, and paused irreso-lute, waiting for an invitation to enter. However, Veronica had many things to think over, and wished to be alone, and reluctantly he said good-bye and turned away.

The little cold wind still blew around Veronica as she went through the shrubbery. She could hear it rustle the boughs behind her as she passed, and saw the unkempt lilacs stir above her head and the leaves come down in a shower. At the window opening upon the terrace she paused, a little spiral of leaves danced in the unswept corners of the steps, and as she opened the unlatched pane, a stream of the fallen Virginia Creeper, scarlet as blood, swept across the floor and rose up in a giddy dance in the eddies before the open fire-place.

Veronica dropped into a big leather-covered armchair and stared at the smouldering fire. The leaves, the draught withdrawn, lay in brilliant patches upon the faded carpet. All was quiet.

Veronica had come to the dividing of the ways, and with a woman's intuition she knew it. She might, by turning her mind towards Butler and the things he stood for, bring back her soul to the normal. But Lucas had shown her the path of the soul from the dark ocean of the Unmanifest to the Cosmic Fire. She had seen, and she could not forget; no soul can. Sooner or later, she knew in her heart, a call would come out of the Unseen, and she must hold herself in readiness to respond to it.

So her moods alternated. A greeting from the gardener, the shouts of playing children down the lane, and she knew that Lucas was dead and buried and the mad dream over. Then the daylight would fade, the wind of evening blow round the house, dancing the leaves into spirals, the dying fire would throw a lessening circle of light about the hearth, and the corners fill with shadows. Then the unseen drew very close to Veronica, and the veil would grow very thin, and through the rifts she would catch brief, shifting glimpses of the great Presences that cast the shadows, and sooner or later, out of the swirlings and speedings of space would come one whom she knew, who would summon her.

Then the old caretaker would bring in the morning paper and Veronica would shake off her dreams and return to realities.

CHAPTER NINE

So Veronica's moods alternated but still she lingered on in the mouldering old house. Meanwhile, Butler assiduously developed the friendship that had begun by the newly-made grave. He would drop in at odd times, the middle of the morning, after tea, after supper, but he would never stop to a meal even were one upon the table. To do so would have occasioned comment in the home circle, and he had no mind that they should know of his visits to the Grange, or its solitary occupant. Veronica, unskilled in the ways of the world, wondered at his refusal, but could not interpret it. Butler was a champion of beauty in distress, but only up to a point; beyond that point, his world bound him.

But nevertheless, in spite of difficulties, he came so often by the secluded wood path that led through the churchyard, that even the mastiff which, chained to a barrel, guarded the back premises, got to know his footstep and ceased to give tongue. Time and again, sitting in the warm lamp-lit room with Veronica, he was on the point of asking her to be his wife, and time and again he hesitated. She would talk freely of her childhood, of the training college, but of her life with Lucas she would tell him no more than she had told the coroner. She had been Mr Lucas's secretary in London when he had managed the affairs of the Society for the Study of Comparative Folk-lore. She had accompanied him to Beckering to continue her duties when he left London. He had been very good to her, and she would permit no aspersion on his memory. Like all the rest of the district,

Butler knew that there was much that these obvious statements did not explain, but Veronica did not offer to enlighten him, and he lacked the courage to put a direct question.

The days drifted by pleasantly enough, he saw just as much of her as if they had been officially engaged, and he was spared all the unpleasantness that publicity would have occasioned. No other male showed any signs of competing, so he was not driven to clinch his bargain from any fear of losing it. Veronica, on her part, adopted an equally drifting policy towards Butler. Although he could well have qualified for the post of Prince Charming and dragon-slayer in the old days, those days were gone for ever, and in the brief stormy interregnum Veronica had known a man in whom the fire of life burnt so fiercely that all other men seemed to her either immature or senile. Lucas alone was a man in his strength. Butler was a child, a puppet. She liked his companionship and was glad that he liked her, but he woke no fire within her.

Things would have continued to drift indefinitely had not Butler come in one day unannounced, to find Veronica nibbling the end of her pen in the effort to cope with some legal-looking documents. His offer of assistance was accepted, and he speedily discovered that he was disentangling the affairs of a considerable estate. This put an entirely different complexion on the matter. Butler did not wish to be mercenary, but the discovery that Veronica had private means, and considerable means too, was certainly a factor to consider.

Butler drew his chair up to the table and helped Veronica to fill in dividend warrants. Though it was sufficiently dark to demand the lamp, his head was perhaps closer to hers than it need have been. A sudden patter of dead leaves struck the glass as a gust of wind set all the windows rattling. They both looked up in astonishment, for the night had been quiet hitherto.

'A storm getting up,' said Butler, and even as he spoke a

105

fresh gust smote the window with renewed vigour. The panes bulged, rocked, and then the crazy fastening gave way. Both panes of the french window burst open, and a great rush of wind laden with a stream of dancing leaves drove into the room. Out went the lamp, but the flames of the logs leaped up as the feathery ashes of the hearth joined the leaves in the wild whirlwind dance of the gale. Butler seized the flanges of the window and forced them shut, then he struck a match and relit the lamp. The renewed light showed scarlet leaves and grey ashes settling slowly down all over the floor. Veronica amid her strewn papers, was staring into space with unseeing eyes. Something of the wild night without seemed to have entered with the rushing wind, and though the uproar had subsided, a lingering spirit of darkness brooded over the room. The lamp gave less light, the fire less heat, and the veil that hides the unseen hung in tatters that the lightest breath might displace. Veronica felt that, should the strange atmosphere that brooded over the room grow the least degree more tangible, something would become visible to the physical eyes of both of them. But Butler, happily oblivious with a wholesome stolidity, gathered up the fallen papers, lit a pipe, and took his seat at the table again to finish the task in hand.

Luckily it was nearly completed, for Veronica found it hard to keep her attention on the documents that demanded her signature. Butler, too, was in a hurry, for supper time was approaching, and he had no wish to draw attention to his movements by being late for the family meal, so the task was speedily dispatched, and he rose to his feet to depart. Veronica, however, was reluctant to let him go, but he resisted all her efforts to persuade him to stay and share her evening meal. She opened the french window and stepped out on to the terrace. To their surprise they found that the wind had died away as suddenly as it had arisen, and no noticeable air was moving in the sheltered garden. Suddenly the piercing howl of a dog's agony cut through the stillness of the valley. The sound came from the outbuildings where the old watch-dog lived and instinctively Butler answered the cry of the animal's distress, dashing round the corner of the terrace at top speed with Veronica close behind him.

They discovered the old mastiff, lying on his side on the flagstones outside the barrel that served him for a kennel. A little foam hung from his dark muzzle and he was panting, otherwise he seemed unharmed. He lifted his head as he became aware of their presence, but dropped it back on the stones again, appearing completely exhausted.

Butler knelt and examined him. 'Poor old chap,' he said. 'He must have had some sort of a fit.' And gathering the heavy dog up in his arms, he managed to bundle him back among the straw of his kennel.

'I wonder what can have been the matter with him,' said Veronica. 'Last night he was howling in the most unaccountable fashion. I have never heard a dog howl quite like that before; a long drawn-out wail on one note. The gardener told me it was the death-howl, and said they were quite upset about it at the cottages down the road; he said that dogs howl like that when they see the souls of the dead passing out.'

'Oh, rubbish Veronica! You don't mean to say you take that seriously?' exclaimed Butler. And he led her round the corner of the house on to the terrace and saw her safely in at the window again before he set out on his walk to the village.

His head was among the stars and his feet scarcely touched the earth as he walked; Veronica was within his reach (it never entered his head that she might not accept him if he proposed), and he whistled Mendelssohn's Wedding March as he went through the darkness of the wood path. As he set foot in the churchyard, the newly-risen moon made lakes of light among the dark yews, and in one such silver pool lay the rough mound of clay that covered the man whose influence still overshadowed the girl of his choice. He paused beside the mound. What secret lay concealed there? He must tackle Veronica straight about that matter; it didn't do to have secrets between man and wife.

'So long,' he said half aloud, nodding to the man that lay below. 'Wish me luck.' And he went on again, whistling.

Veronica, left alone at the Grange, ate her solitary supper and then sat over the fire, gazing into the flames and reviewing her life. Her childhood on the Surrey hills where nothing ever happened; the strain of her life at the training school; her association with Lucas, when altogether too much happened; and now her strange tie to this dismantled, sodden place where he had died. Then her mind turned to Butler. She knew quite well that he would soon ask her to marry him. If it had not been for Lucas, she would have liked him very much. He was big; handsome in his blond way, and good natured. He had already adopted little proprietary ways towards her which she rather liked. But behind him loomed the dark personality of Lucas, and though Butler would have appealed to the girl she used to be before she went to the house in the Bloomsbury square, a side of her nature had been awakened to life that he could neither comprehend nor satisfy.

Lucas had gone out prematurely, in the prime of his strength, his work unfinished, and all his desires focused upon this earth, and she knew he would return if it were within his power. Forgotten was her terror of Lucas in the Bloomsbury days, she only remembered the man of the final forty-eight hours, she only felt the strange bond that existed between them.

As she pondered, a sound upon the gravel outside drew her attention. A shadow came up to the uncurtained window and stood looking in, and she saw that it was the old mastiff who had got loose from his kennel and now stood gazing into the lighted room, his eyes gleaming green with the reflection of the lamp. These strange, incandescent eyes put her in mind of Lucas when he hypnotized her, his eyes seemed to shine with an inner light in just the same way; in fact, Lucas seemed very close to her tonight.

She had no fear of the dog; dogs were her passion, and she was in two minds about inviting him in when he settled the matter for himself by rearing up on his hind legs and setting his fore-paws against the window. The crazy fastenings gave way and in he came, a great brindled beast, the black of his muzzle touched with white, for he was an old dog.

Veronica crossed the room and closed the window behind him, for the night was cold. The dog walked over to the fire and stood upon the hearth rug looking round the room; he did not wander about sniffing, after the custom of dogs in a strange place, but, using his eyes rather than his nose, he turned his head from side to side, surveying his surroundings, and especially Veronica.

She returned to her seat by the fire, and he came and stood before her, gazing into her face with his brown dog's eyes. She leant forward and returned his gaze. 'What was it you howled at last night?' she said. The dog blew out his nostrils and woofed heavily, and a clumsy paw scrabbled at her skirt. He came nearer and laid his heavy black jowl on her knee. She bent down, looking straight into his eyes. 'If you meet Mr Lucas again, tell him I want to see him.'

The dog gave a great woof, as if of relief, and sat down on his haunches. His mouth opened, his red tongue came out, and he grinned as only a dog can grin. Veronica did not quite like that grin; there was something sinister in the way this dumb animal was laughing at her. 'Lie down,' she said, indicating the hearth rug, and obediently he disposed himself as she had directed. She herself took up some fancywork, and the dog lay at her feet, motionless but watching every movement, till bedtime came and she rose.

'Come along,' she said to her companion, 'I must fasten you up for the night.' He followed her to the window, and laying a hand on his massive neck, she guided him back to the yard, the great creature padding beside her upon silent feet. There she discovered that he had escaped from his chain by slipping his head out of his collar, so she discreetly drew the strap one hold tighter, for she did not like the idea of this great dog being at liberty. True, he had shown himself a friendly enough creature, but his silent appearance at the window had had in it something of the sinister. She returned to the lamp-lit sitting-room but it seemed as if a darkness had entered during her absence. The flickering flames of the wood fire, now rising, now falling as the logs stirred in their burning, cast fitful gleams into the darkness and Veronica hastened upstairs away from those ill-omened shadows.

In the morning her nervousness seemed ridiculous. She still shrank from the idea of the mastiff being free to roam about the house. He was a large and powerful dog and would be a very ugly customer should his present good-will be changed to resentment. After breakfast Veronica went to pay him a visit to see if he suffered any after-effects from his curious indisposition of the night before. He did not come out to greet her, and it was not until she knelt down at the entrance to his barrel that a head was thrust out in response to her summons. A pair of misty eyes blinked dazedly at the sunlight, then the head was withdrawn again and no appeals of hers could induce it to reappear, though the eyes glowed with a strange green animal fire out of the darkness. The whole 'feel' of dog, kennel, and surroundings was so repellent that she drew hastily back and hurried away from the yard and its sinister occupant.

By the time she had reached the lawn in front of the terrace she was half minded to return; it was ridiculous to feel like this about the dog. The previous evening she had quite liked the friendly old thing, and anyway, the animal was obviously ailing. Seeing the gardener among the shrubs, she went over and spoke to him concerning the dog's condition, and he told her that the animal had refused its food that morning, but that he did not care for the task of examining it single-handed. There was a very good vet.

in the village, however, and if Miss Mainwaring liked, he would ask him to come round and have a look at it.

Wrapping herself in Lucas's coat, which had become her regular wear now that the weather had turned colder, Veronica went for a walk down by the river-side. Her walk took her past the row of labourers' cottages that stood a little way down the lane. Several children were playing outside who regarded her with an awed curiosity, and of the glances she received through the open door from their elders, some were pitying and some were hostile. Veronica passed on; their opinions did not trouble her.

She could not make up her mind concerning Alec. Her old self would have been well enough content with his easy, pleasant surfaces, but her present self had known Lucas, and she was torn between her two selves. Should she wish to become again the Veronica of the Surrey hills, then her way of return lay by the path that Butler was opening before her. She had penetrated into the hidden kingdom, and only a close union with a dweller in the outer world could draw her back. All this she knew by means of an inner intuition that day by day was growing stronger. She remembered the great Hand that had closed behind her the gates of the invisible world, sealing them with the Sign of the Cross. She had been forbidden to seek that world again, but now in a strange, subtle way it seemed to be approaching her; impalpably, imperceptibly.

All Veronica's early training, the influence of her home life, her religious teaching, had bade her forget the macabre dream of the past months and return to the healthy normal life symbolized by Butler. But she had known Lucas, and she could not forget. He had opened up to her soul wide vistas down which go the paths that lead over the horizon. She could never settle down within the small circle of protecting walls that would be drawn around her should she cast in her lot with Alec. But Veronica knew that should she remain by herself, then, step by step, she would be drawn deeper into the unseen world of whose heights and

111

depths she had hitherto had but fugitive glimpses. It was this dread that made her try to see all the best that was in Butler and what he had to offer, as an alternative to the heights and horrors that Lucas, even though dead, seemed still to be able to open up to her.

It was these thoughts that made her bestow upon Alec her rare, slow, Mona Lisa smile as she opened the window to admit him when he came to see her that evening, and this smile swung the keystone of his resolution into place.

'Veronica,' he said, 'do you know what I have come for?' He looked down into her big, grey-blue eyes, and a twinge of doubt assailed him. Her eyes were veiled, remote, something lay behind them that was hidden from him. There were depths in this girl that he could not comprehend. 'Veronica,' he said, 'I want you to be my wife.'

She did not answer. Chin on hand, she sat motionless, gazing into the fire. Among the coals her imagination pictured the face of Lucas.

A faint sound from the other side of the room roused her; a dead leaf, borne by some wandering current of air, had drifted across the window-sill and fallen upon the polished wood within.

'Damn that window,' exclaimed Butler, and, crossing the room in his heavy shooting boots, he shut it noisily. Returning to the hearth, he took his stand before the girl once more. 'Well, Veronica,' he said. 'What is it to be?'

To Veronica, a cold, invisible darkness seemed to have flown into the room while the window was open. Her old terror of the Unseen returned to her with renewed force, and, turning to Butler she held out both her hands. But as she looked into his eyes, a sudden knowledge came to her that she had nothing to give him, for her soul had followed another man out into the darkness. Looking over his head, she saw that the shadows from the corners of the room were closing in about the hearth, and her grip suddenly tightened upon the hands that held hers.

She rose unsteadily to her feet. 'I must have time to

think,' she said. 'Come back tomorrow morning, and I will give you your answer.'

He straightened himself beside her, and catching her in his arms, he kissed her. For an instant a vision of Lucas's face, distorted with rage, appeared before Veronica's eyes. Butler released her. 'Bye,' he said. 'I'll be round bright and early.'

Securing the window behind him, she stood listening to his departing footsteps, heavy upon the gravel. He reached the edge of the wood, and the sounds ceased as he set foot upon the soft earth path. Suddenly Veronica's heart stood still; silent and swift-moving as a shadow, the mastiff passed the window, nose to ground, hot upon the scent of the retreating man.

Veronica, her senses paralysed, leant up against the window-frame for support. Should she cry out to warn him? Should she snatch up some weapon and go after him? Should she run to the cottages for help? Even as she debated, there rang out upon the night air a cry, wild, appalling, cut short in the middle. Then there was silence. Veronica's knees gave under her, and she dropped in a huddled heap into a near-by chair.

For a time she lay with her head buried in the cushions. Then she lifted it. Eyes straining into the darkness, she waited. An uncertain shadow moved upon the lawn, and then a heavy head rose above the steps that led to the terrace, and the dog stood without.

A rope of dark-coloured foam hung from his muzzle, and his flanks heaved. He was an old dog, and the struggle had tried him. The eyes of the girl stared into the dog's, those of the animal filled with a strange phosphorescence. He reared up on his hind legs and placed a paw on the window-pane. Veronica watched with a helpless fascination as the crazy woodwork bulged inwards till the catch slipped and the window burst open. A pair of brindled shoulders filled the aperture and paused, as if waiting for an invitation. Veron-

113

ica made neither sound nor movement, and the animal entered.

It came up to her and rested its muzzle upon her knee. Still she made no movement; a strange paralysis held her motionless. A sense of her feeling towards it seemed to communicate itself to the dog's mind, for the hair upon its neck rose in anger and a low growl came from between its teeth. Then, as Veronica watched, the pupils of its eyes slowly contracted till two disks of greenish-brown, opaque as china, looked back at her. The face of a man superimposed itself upon the face of the dog; old, forgotten tales of were-wolves came to her, of creatures, half animal, half human, the bodies of beasts ensouled by magicians, a tangle of fairy tales and ghost stories raced through her mind.

Then Veronica fainted. When she recovered, the dog had gone, but the window still stood open. With shaking hands she secured it, and then, dazed and numb, dragged herself up to her room.

CHAPTER TEN

Veronica woke to find warm autumn sunlight streaming into her room and her ears filled with the song of the birds. For a moment her spirits rose up, and then a shadow fell across them as she remembered Lucas. He was not dead; she knew that much with a certain inner conviction. Moreover, he had not abandoned his pursuit of her, she knew that also. Somewhere, close to her though invisible, spirit of outer darkness that he was, he came in the cold eddying wind that tossed up the dead leaves in a spiral dance and strong enough to burst open the frail fastenings of the french window and cast her papers to the floor as if with the sweep of an angry hand.

She saw it all so clearly now. Lucas, the disembodied mind unable to manifest, unable to materialize save in fleeting and unstable forms, yet fully aware of all that transpired, was actuated by the same unscrupulous will that had carried him through life. Urged on by who knows what devils of jealous hate and frustrated longing, he had seized upon and obsessed the body of the dog. In the old days in the Bloomsbury square Veronica found herself moving in a world that was as mad as a lunatic's dream. The invisible collar that Lucas had put about her neck was a commonplace phenomenon of suggestion, had she but known it; but what of this dog with the eyes and purpose of a man? No longer, however, did she think of him as the man towards whom her heart had softened, rather he was once again the man of dark and unknown purposes who had used her unscrupulously for his own ends. Lucas would drag her with him to the darkness could he once lay hands upon her soul – and alone in her sunlit bedroom, she shivered as if the chill of that darkness were already about her.

She did not remain alone long however; the old caretaker appeared, and by gestures rather than speech intimated that someone was below who wished to see her. Dressing hastily, Veronica descended to the shuttered hall of the old mansion; there she found two men, one of whom she knew, but the other was a stranger. The former was the doctor who had been called in when Lucas was found dead; but he was also the father of Alec, and from his presence Veronica guessed that the odium of the whole terrible affair would be laid at her door. Powerless to defend herself, to offer any explanation, or to make known the real state of affairs, she fell back upon the tactics of the inquest. Her interlocutors knew perfectly well that there was more in the matter than their questioning could lay bare. They also felt, and the doctor, for his part, showed it very plainly, that the two deaths were in some way connected, and that Veronica was at the bottom of them, and his attitude towards her could not have shown greater detestation if he had caught her red-handed. His companion, obviously uncomfortable at this manifestation of hate, stood switching his riding-boots uneasily with a hunting-crop, and staring at this girl, the subject of so much local rumour, whom he now met face to face for the first time.

Veronica, for her part, merely stated any facts that were required of her, offering no comment upon them, well knowing that neither of these men could hit upon the hidden links that bound the whole affair together.

Finally, the cross-examination having elicited nothing save that Butler was a regular visitor at the Grange (Veronica spared her interlocutor the information that his son had proposed marriage), the man, baffled and angry, turned to

116

his companion and exclaimed, 'Well, Hargreaves, what do you make of this extraordinary affair?'

For the first time the other man spoke: 'If you want my opinion, doctor, there is nothing mysterious about it, it is just a plain case of hydrophobia, and the best thing to do is to dispose of the dog so that he can't infect any others. The only thing that isn't plain is, how a chained-up beast like that got it in the first place? I suppose you have no objection to my destroying him, Miss Mainwaring? It has got to be done, and I will do it quite painlessly. I am the vet, you know.'

Veronica bowed her head. 'Do as you please,' she said. 'Only bury him a long way off, and deep,' and she turned away into the billiard room.

For a time she sat alone, staring into space. Lucas, who had drawn so near, seemed very remote at the present moment. She wondered what would happen to him when they destroyed his dog-form. Would he be able to pick up his contact with her again when forced out of this, his present refuge?

Even as she mused, a wild hullabaloo broke out in the kitchen. Someone, feminine, was having violent hysterics, and her shrieks rose high above a chorus of male voices raised in consternation. Veronica ran down the long passage that led to the back premises, and there found the old caretaker laid out upon the floor and shrieking at the full pitch of her lungs; a number of white-faced rustics drew back at Veronica's entrance, eyeing her askance.

'What is the matter?' demanded the girl, confronting them.

No one replied, and the group faded away through the half-opened door. Spying the inevitable small boy in the yard, watching proceedings, Veronica darted out and caught him by his ragged jacket before he could escape.

'What happened?' she demanded of him.

'They shot the dog, miss,' he replied writhing in her grasp.

'I know that, but what are they all so frightened of? It is no use wriggling, I won't let you go till you tell me.'

'It – it was the gentleman, miss,' said the boy in a husky whisper. 'He's come back.'

'What gentleman?' demanded Veronica.

'The dark gentleman, who was here with you, miss. He came out of the kennel when they shot the dog, I seed 'un myself, we all seed 'n; he came out of the kennel, and he stood up there in the sunlight, as plain as plain could be, grinnin' at us, and then he faded away like a puff of smoke, a bit at a time, like, till he was all gone. But I seed 'un, and we all seed 'un. Let me go, miss,' and with a final squirm he shot out of Veronica's hands and escaped.

Veronica returned to the billiard room but even as she opened the door, she was aware that someone awaited her. She looked round but there was no one there. Crossing the room, she stepped out through the french windows on to the terrace, and almost without realizing what she was doing, held it open for the one who followed. 'So you have come back?' she said.

She waited, as if expecting a reply, but none came. Then she spoke again. 'I cannot forgive what you did to Alec Butler, nor this matter of the dog. I can forgive what you did to me, that was over and forgotten, but the dog was horrible, and I cannot forgive that.'

Silence fell again. Veronica had said what she had to say, but no reply could reach her senses. She turned, recrossed the gravel path, entered the french window, and shut it quickly behind her. Then she stood watching. The day was still and sunny, but presently, as she expected, the dead leaves lying in the angles of the steps began to be stirred by a little breeze. They rose up in the grip of a miniature whirlwind and smote upon the pane. The window bulged inwards, the crazy catch slipping, but Veronica put her hand on the frame and thrust it home again, then she set a heavy armchair against it. The leaves, tossed all over the terrace by the last indignant gust, slowly settled down again, baffled.

From that time onwards Veronica seldom knew what it was to be alone. It was just like the old days, Lucas was somewhere about. The vividness of the impression varied however. During bright sunlight she would be immune from his influence, but on a grey day, and especially as dusk crept on, the presence would grow increasingly tangible, till, with the onset of darkness, Lucas himself was beside her. She could see nothing, hear nothing, no shred of communication reached her yet she felt the very moods of his temperament.

Having at last succeeded in making her aware of his presence his powers seemed to be increasing. Whether she was growing more psychic, or he more adept at bending matter to his will, she did not know – but certainly a rapport had been set up between her mind and his, and certainly that rapport was growing.

Veronica, knowing Lucas to be evil, and feeling herself in his power, that dark presence was the consummation of all the horrors of nightmare. Though she knew his methods, she could not divine his thoughts, and it was some little time before she discovered that hers could be read by him with the greatest readiness. If she allowed her thoughts to wander to Alec the atmosphere in her immediate vicinity filled with a menacing anger, and time and again the whirlwind dance of the leaves would toss themselves up in their impotent displeasure. But if, on the other hand, she allowed her thoughts to dwell upon the few short hours of companionship and sympathy that had preceded Lucas's death then the room glowed with a strange warmth that seemed to wrap itself about her form in a mantle of invisible light.

Veronica gradually learnt to know the moods of her unseen visitor, and soon the presence, which at first had had for her all the horror of the unknown, became familiar and

119

was accepted more or less as a matter of course. Though she still dreaded it, she feared it no more than she had feared the man, and as time went on, his old uncanny fascination began to assert itself again. She found herself watching for his approach as the light faded, and in some curious, subconscious way, lending herself to his manifestation. She dreaded him, yet she would have missed him had he not appeared.

It was towards All Hallows Eve that he at last succeeded in crossing the boundary of the unmanifest. A bright frosty day had tempted Veronica to a long walk, and coming in as dusk fell, she had been glad to fling her weary body into a big armchair by the hearth and doze in the fire-lit room. There, every muscle relaxed, she lay back among the cushions, between sleeping and waking, her eyes gazing steadily into the heart of the glowing coals. Suddenly she felt that swift swoop into outer space that had always heralded her departure upon the strange journeys of the soul on which Lucas had dispatched her. This time, however, oblivion did not close upon her; instead, she remained aware of her surroundings, although all power of movement seemed to be inhibited. For a while she lay thus, in a dreamy, somnolent state that was not unpleasant. Then a new sensation made itself felt, as if something were being drawn out of her left side, at first a trickling, then a strange draining sensation, and she saw a white, mistlike pool accumulating at her feet. Slowly the pool spread out, rose up, took form in front of her, and then a face began to form, and it was the face of Lucas!

Veronica, drained of vitality, lay back in her chair, and saw the dead man take life before her. This strange manifestation did not last many moments; Lucas dared not prolong it; and in a few seconds the devitalized girl felt life flowing back into her, and simultaneously, saw the form before her shrink, lose outline, and subside into an amorphous pool of mist at her feet. Then she awoke as from a dream, asking herself whether this strange experience had any existence outside her imagination.

After supper it seemed even more unreal, and when she awoke from a heavy dreamless sleep in the morning, all but a vague memory had vanished. The day passed slowly by in minor tasks until Veronica suddenly remembered a letter to her lawyer that demanded an answer. Sitting down to the writing table, she took her pen and then fell to nibbling the end of it, for she was not a fluent correspondent, and business matters had ever been beyond her. Having written 'Dear Sir,' she stuck fast, pen poised above paper, when, to her surprise, she saw a line of writing slowly trace itself across the blank white page.

'How are you, Veronica? Justin writing.'

The girl stared in amazement at the words that slowly formed themselves under her eyes. The pen, without volition of hers, had written; the writing, though done by her hand, was not her usual script, yet it was curiously familiar. It was a man's hand, and Justin was a man's name. She knew no one called Justin, yet, in some odd way, it sounded familiar. Then she remembered, it was the name of the Roman Lucas had told her about, the man who had loved and lost a girl in the days of that ancient, world-wide empire.

'Exactly. Justinian was his name, and Justin is my name, the English version of the Latin word, only perhaps you know me better as J. Lucas.'

Again the hand had written without her volition, and Veronica sat transfixed, gazing at the words that formed themselves upon the paper, so aptly answering her unspoken thought.

Once again the writing commenced. 'You will stand by me, won't you, Veronica? I am depending on you, you know.' Then, as if divining with that shrewd mind of his the line of appeal that would influence her: 'If you do not help me, I am lost.'

Veronica, whose first thought had been panic-stricken flight out into the garden, remained motionless, listening,

121

waiting.

Again the pen began to move, and her eyes followed the writing.

'You did very well last night. The subtle ethers are easily detached from your dense body, and I can draw them out and build myself a form with them, but I am afraid it will be too much of a strain for you to do it often by yourself. The only thing I can suggest is that I form a partial materialization from you, and then we get as close as we can to some other people, and I pick up the rest of the stuff I want from them. I think I can manage it if we wait till they are asleep.'

Veronica flung down her pen, hastily opened the window, and went out on to the terrace. What horrible experiment was the dead man contemplating? She was entirely ignorant of these things, even her imagination had never envisaged the strange forces Lucas employed nor the yet stranger aims and affairs that occupied his attention. Lucas was no more dead than she was, he was merely without a body, and was evidently bent upon supplying the deficiency by whatever means he could bend to his purpose.

Soon the gathering darkness and bitter wind drove her within doors, and the evening passed rapidly away to bedtime. Suddenly the Presence was in the room, she could feel it at her elbow. Slowly she sank back into the chair from which she had risen, and as she sank back, the downward rush of the soul into space commenced. Once again the strange substance which was her life flowed from her left side and drew itself out and again Lucas's eyes looked out at her from the folds of its whiteness. But here the process was arrested, condensation went no further, only the eyes were fully materialized; the rest of the form hung like a wreath of smoke upon the air.

Veronica, still in full possession of her faculties, felt strangely light and detached. Slowly she rose from her chair and stood before him, compelled, yet eager to do his will. Following him, she moved over to a corner of the room

122

where the old trench-coat lay over a chair, and drew it round her shoulders.

The eyes shone with an uncanny light, half tenderness, half triumph, and as the grey form moved over to the window, Veronica moved after it, and on the heels of the drifting mist-like form she moved swiftly down the darkened terrace.

A tenuous silver cord of vapour connected her with the gliding shadow ahead, and she knew that at all costs that cord must be kept intact. Then she noticed another and still stranger phenomenon, pitch dark though it was, she could see quite plainly in a leaden-grey twilight. To her, the landscape was illuminated with a peculiar livid light and yet no shadows were thrown by any object.

They moved with swift, effortless speed down the weedgrown driveway and out into the road on the river-bank, and then turned to the left, and Veronica guessed that their objective was the row of labourers' cottages that stood a little way down the lane. Hardly daring to breathe, she followed the shadowy form that drew her by the silver cord till both she and her half-seen guide halted under the wall of the nearest cottage.

For a moment the dark pools of the eyes were turned towards her, and then, like a wreath of smoke, the form rose into the air above her head, and she saw that it was pressing itself against the small leaded panes that hung in the crazy window-frame up under the cottage eaves. Some crack must have been found, for the drifting mist slowly disappeared till nothing but the tenuous silver trail was left that connected it with her own body.

For an eternity she waited, no sound issuing from the cottages, and then she heard a faint creaking as the casement above her head was opened and a hand appeared upon the window-sill. An amorphous mist had drifted in through the crack, but it was a distinctly physical form that came out, and from the thud with which it struck the ground, Veronica knew that it must have a certain amount

123

of weight. Then it came towards her over the rank winter vegetation, and she saw, swathed and cowled in soft grey drapery, the figure of Lucas as she had known him in life.

Slipping his hand though her arm in the old familiar gesture, he led her swiftly down the lane by which they had come, and back through the garden to the terrace.

Wood-ash still glowed redly on the hearth in the billiard room, and Veronica, seizing the poker, would have stirred it into flame, for she was perished with cold and fear, when a hand that was entirely tangible was laid upon her arm, and a familiar voice said in her ear: 'Steady, child, I cannot stand much light.'

With that authoritative touch of his he led her unresisting back to her chair, and there, as she lay among the cushions, he bent over her.

'Now I am going to give back to you what I have borrowed. It will not be safe to keep you too long in your present condition,' and even as he spoke the words, Veronica felt the returning flow of the vital forces that had been partially withdrawn. This time, however, the figure before her did not entirely dematerialize. When she returned to waking consciousness, there remained of the erstwhile tangible form a drifting mist marked by dark pools of blackness where there had been eyes. That which he had taken from the sleeping people in the cottages he had retained.

The floating form drew near as if to take farewell of her, and then, gliding over to the window, slowly drifted forth through an aperture in the rotting frame, while Veronica, dazed and exhausted, struck a light and surveyed the now empty room.

CHAPTER ELEVEN

The next morning Veronica felt the whole transaction to be a bad dream when a pair of soaked and mud-stained slippers caught her eyes, but still she refused to admit the possibility of reality. After breakfast she was taking her morning walk along the lane on the river bank, when a sound of wheels behind her made her look round, and there was the doctor, Alec's father, driving along the grass-grown roadway. He gave her one glance, and drove swiftly past without any other sign of recognition than that look of hate and repulsion. This man had not been able to assign any other cause of death than heart failure in the case of Lucas, nor of haemorrhage of the jugular vein from dog-bite in the case of his son, yet his intuition told him that in some way Veronica was connected with these happenings and he hated her without reason but with an unerring instinct.

Veronica continued her walk down the over-grown lane, and presently reached the row of labourers' cottages that had been the scene of her dream of the previous night. Even by daylight she could not cast off the horror of that memory; its shadow still hung about her. There was the angle of the rose-covered porch where she had stood; and there, up under the eaves, the little window by which Lucas had entered.

A sound attracted her attention and the doctor himself stood at the gate of the first cottage observing her intently. 'A child died in that cottage last night, and four others are seriously ill,' he said. 'They were quite all right when they

125

went to bed.'

They stood looking into each other's eyes, neither able to offer any comment. The little cold wind, now so familiar, sprang up, and a great drift of autumn leaves swept across the roadway. Veronica gave an apologetic, frightened, helpless little shrug and walked slowly away. The doctor paused, irresolute, uncertain for a moment whether to pursue her, and then he shook his head angrily and went back into the cottage.

Returning to the Grange Veronica faced the issue. It was useless to regard the happenings as a bad dream any longer. There in the cottage a child lay dead, and four others sick. Such was the price that had to be paid that a dead man might live even such shadowy life as Lucas had achieved. Lucas, remorseless individualist that he was, stole from those who could offer least defence – young children. Veronica remembered the little new-made graves that she had seen when she visited the churchyard, and wondered how many lives had been sacrificed in order that Lucas might keep his footing on the physical plane.

Of one thing she was quite determined, however, no more little children should be harmed if it were in her power to prevent it. There was a very great deal of the mother instinct in Veronica, and Lucas could not have found a surer way of making her turn at bay than by attacking children. She would lend herself to no more materializations that could be turned to such ghastly purposes. As the day wore on she waited the coming of dusk, knowing full well that it would bring Lucas, and she prepared herself for the contest that she knew must ensue. What line he would take with her, she did not know, but upon one thing she was doggedly determined; she would not leave the room, and she shrewdly suspected that if she wouldn't, Lucas couldn't, owing to the tenuous silver cord that united them when materialization took place. What Lucas would do to her by way of retaliation Veronica did not know, and strangely enough, had ceased to care.

Darkness set in early that night, for the sunset had been veiled in clouds, and hardly had the last light gone before Veronica was aware of the shadowy cowled figure with the dark flashing eyes that seemed to build itself out of the shadows. Apparently Lucas had now got enough ectoplasm gathered together to enable him to manifest at will, provided the light was dim enough, but not enough for speech or any definite action. More of this strange subtle substance had to be obtained from somewhere and Veronica was determined that he should not have it. How he was to be prevented was another matter, but she was determined that he should not have her co-operation.

She knew that they were embarked upon a trial of strength, and braced her whole being to meet it. The dark eyes among the grey drapery showed that their owner was well aware of this change of attitude on her part; they looked surprised, reproachful, but the anger that Veronica had expected was absent.

The sensation of the swift downward swoop with which she was now so familiar passed through Veronica's nerves, and once again she saw the mist-like substance flow from her that should turn Lucas into the semblance of a living man. Not much was needed for this accomplishment now, and in a condition very near her normal consciousness Veronica saw Lucas materialize before her.

There he stood in the dim red glow of the coals, swathed and cowled in soft grey drapery, but the hands looked as if they could grip, and the face showed the colour of life under its dark skin.

The process having gone as far as Lucas dared to carry it, they faced each other, the man partly materialized, and the girl partly dematerialized.

'Well, Veronica, are you pleased to see me?'

She made him no answer. Great as was her horror of him, and of the strange conditions of his reappearing, yet he still had a fascination for her. This he seemed to divine, for the shadowy lips curved into a smile.

'Not altogether displeased? We are coming along, Veronica.'

There was a pause while they studied each other. Veronica noted the way he had concentrated such substance as was available for his use in the upper parts of his form; head, shoulders, and hands were well materialized, but the lower limbs tailed off in a long floating wisp of drapery.

Then the man spoke again. 'Now, the next thing is to finish the process we began last night. I have marked down a house on the other side of the village that I want to go to, and if you will put on some shoes we will make a start.'

But Veronica did not stir, and the dark eyes among the shadowy drapery opened wide in amazement, for, practised hypnotist that he was, Lucas had never before had experience of a subject who went easily into trance and then proved unamenable to suggestion. He did not know that Veronica had 'gone off' with her mind concentrated upon the idea that she would not leave the room, and that this prior auto-suggestion would nullify all subsequent commands. Within the limits of the four walls she was his to command at will, but outside the four walls neither he nor anyone else could make her go.

Baffled by the turn affairs had taken, Lucas shifted his ground.

'Aren't you going to help me?' he said.

Veronica, motionless in her chair as a statue, turned her face towards him as if the closed eyes had sight.

'One of those children is dead,' she said; 'and the others are very ill.'

'I am sorry the child is dead,' said Lucas. 'I must have taken more from it than it could stand. The others will be all right in a day or two; they will soon pick up again.'

'There have been several children who have died from what you did to them,' said Veronica.

'Have there? Children die very easily; such a small withdrawal of vitality seems to deplete them.'

'There won't be any more,' answered Veronica.

'No, I hope not,' said Lucas. 'But come, now, we want to make a start. I think one more expedition will do the trick.'

'There will not be another expedition,' said Veronica.

'Oh yes, there will,' said Lucas, and the dark brows met in a frown under the grey hooded draperies as he concentrated upon her. The hand, long-fingered and flat-palmed as in life, shot out towards her and passed with a slow stroking movement down across her face. Veronica's body did not stir, but down again into the dark blue abyss sank her soul as the hypnotic trance deepened under Lucas's manipulations.

Again he essayed to command her upon this deeper level of trance, and again her mind, set to a keynote, resisted. Yet again he sent her swooping to a still lower level, and yet again she eluded him. Then, angered and baffled beyond caution, he thrust her out a third time, when, to his surprise, the rigidity left her figure, and she sank back among the cushions like a child asleep, a look of wonderful peace taking the place of the strained, anxious expression of her face. For Lucas had over-reached himself. He had thrust Veronica out beyond any plane upon which he himself could function. She had escaped from his control; her soul had passed from the subjective condition of hypnotic trance and become objective upon a higher plane of consciousness; subconsciousness had given place to superconsciousness, and Veronica had escaped. Her soul, hounded deeper and yet deeper into the subjective state, had suddenly broken through and had gone to its own place and was among its own kind.

A smile parted Veronica's lips, and she seemed to be answering a greeting. Lucas, watching her, knew that she had passed to those regions for the right of entrance to which he had sold his soul. Something in her own nature had given her the key to the gate that was barred to him. He watched and waited, unable to follow her where she had gone. He remembered the time when an unknown Power had intervened on her behalf upon the road to Brighton, striking him down with the sudden impact of force. Lucas asked himself what manner of soul it was that functioned through the child-like personality of Veronica. Of ancient lineage and high initiation it must be in order to contact these levels.

The immortal soul overshadowed rather than incarnated in the body of Veronica Mainwaring, and the personality built up by the experiences of a single life had hitherto given but little indication of that which lay behind it. He guessed that she had no need to incarnate upon her own account; earth had no lessons to teach a soul of this type, her place was elsewhere. He might have guessed this from her desire-lessness and lack of all resentment. Why, then, was she here at all? Some tie held her bound; some link yet remained between her and this plane of existence. Lucas was well aware that in past lives they had trodden the same path and worked together at the same occult work. There is no stronger bond than this; it will hold when the cords of love and hate are loosened. Lucas had lost track of her after that last fateful incarnation at Avignon, when she had definitely chosen the White, and he the Black Path, and had paid with his life for his choice.

Lucas waited impatiently while Veronica's soul wandered in the regions of light whither he could not penetrate. The shadows were his kingdom, and the dark waters of the abyss whence elemental substance can be drawn. She woke from her trance as naturally as a child from sleep to find the room glowing with a strange warmth. She was alone, but the aroma of Lucas's presence hung about the room readily perceptible to her hyper-sensitized condition. Somewhere, in the stormy night outside he was tossed and buffeted by the winds of space. He who had defied the laws of life was caught in their cross-currents, and the great smooth flow of evolution was twisted into a maelstrom as he sought to deflect its tides to his petty personal ends.

Veronica was aware of a curious sense of buoyancy and

freedom. Life pulsed within her, and yet she was heavy with sleep, and with unsteady feet went up to bed.

She awoke in the morning conscious of having dreamt. Yet somehow these dreams were not as other dreams, a type she had never known before. And yet they were vaguely familiar; like forgotten childhood memories. Somewhere, at some time, she had known those tall, slow-moving figures, distinguished by the colours of their cloaks; somewhere she had heard the deep resonant tones of their speech, and their language was not strange to her. One of them had told her to place herself in his hands and trust him. She was to trust unreservedly, and she would be guided. Something was to be made plain to her, someone was to be sent, but who, and what, remained obscure. Broad general impressions lingered in her mind but details eluded her. She gathered that the struggle she had hitherto waged unaided had been taken in hand by higher powers. She was no longer alone and unfriended. Solitary though her life might appear, the unseen was close about her and she was aware of it.

She queried persistently the reality of last night's experience, but there was no means by which she could test its truth. In her memory there lingered a feeling that she had found her way into some great organization that had branches upon many planes of existence, and that its members would come to her assistance in case of need.

The day passed away uneventfully, Lucas's hour had not yet come, it was not till after dark that he could function. Veronica knew the time of his manifestation, and awaited him. As before, the deepening of the twilight heralded his arrival, and with the passing of the last light a presence made itself known in the room. Again the same process was repeated, the available life forces were divided, till these two met upon common ground, half-way between the unseen and the seen.

The cowled figure formed itself and spoke: 'Veronica,

131

we must come to an understanding. Are you going to help me or not?'

Veronica faccd him as she had often faced him in life. 'I will do anything I can to help you,' she said. 'But you shall not do that ghastly thing to the children again if I can prevent it.'

'What else can I do?' said the cowled figure. 'If I do not replenish my vitality I cannot hold even this form together, and then I go to the Second Death. You do not know what that is, do you, Veronica?'

She shook her head, 'I know nothing about these things.'

'Just as well for you. But I can tell you this, I do not wish to go to that Second Death!'

In his urgency he swayed towards her, and a hand that was as real as in life was laid upon her arm.

Veronica put out her hand, and the soft smooth draperies under her touch were like no textile she had ever felt. 'I do not want to do you any harm, Mr Lucas, but I cannot let you hurt those children. It is all so horrible. Why must these things be?'

'Because they cannot be helped,' answered the man. 'I have got to feed or die, and I don't propose to die if I can help it.'

'But you *are* dead,' cried Veronica.

'There is no such thing as death in the way you mean,' answered the man. 'I am alive, very much alive, and if I can once succeed in building myself a machine, I will live as you live. But at present I am only half-way there, I must have more life, and I have got to take it where I can get it.'

'You shall not take it from the children again,' said Veronica. 'What I can do for you I will do, but the children you shall not have.' She faced him: young, and even for her years curiously immature. Veronica moved blindly, as her instincts prompted her, but Lucas knew what forces they were that drove her. 'I do not understand these things, Mr Lucas, but I am willing to do whatever I can to help you, I am not afraid; and although I do not understand them, I seem to know something about them.'

'I dare say you do,' said Lucas. 'And you will know more before you have finished. There is only one thing I ask of you, to lend me enough of your subtle ethers to enable me to collect material for a body through which I can function, and if you will not do that, then there is nothing to be done, we are at a deadlock.'

'I am willing to lend you my forces,' said Veronica. 'But I will not let you touch the children.'

'And it is only from the children that I am strong enough at present to take the forces right out and keep them,' he answered. 'If I persist in drawing upon your forces, I shall draw you over to my phase of existence – death in life – Veronica, and even I draw the line at that. You won't let me come to you, and I won't draw you over to me. So there we are, and I hope you can see a way out of it, for I cannot.'

Veronica had no answer to offer. The grey form before her swayed like the blown flame of a candle as emotions that were still human coursed through it.

Lucas spoke again. 'If I did not love you it would not matter, but I love you, and I cannot do this thing. If I had not cared what happened to you, I could have let the brethren strike you and escaped myself as I had always intended to, but when it came to the point I couldn't do it.'

The room, dimly lit by the dying fire, was a cave of darkness. The lamp was unlit, and the fire seemed repressed and made sinister by the presence of this being who had intruded upon a world where he had no right to be. Something of his nature had entered into the fire and influenced its burning. It was no longer the cheery hearth of human comfort, but a flickering witch-light that ministered to spells. Lucas, when he returned from the unseen, did not come alone, but a multitude of others slipped through the door that opened to admit him. Beings of another order of life.

The thinning of the veil had set up a process of spiritual

osmosis, and the more vigorous forms of the unseen were beginning to absorb the life of the plane of manifestation. Lucas had known all along that herein lay the danger. By refusing to pass on to the place appointed he had taken up his abode in the antechamber between the unseen and the seen, the realm of that which had no form, whence the root-substance of matter was drawn and to which it would return when the ensouling life had outworn it. Herein functioned creatures of another order of creation whose nearest analogy was in the saprophytic life of the bacteria; the scavengers of creation. They had their place in its processes, but, when they obtruded beyond their appointed sphere, they were the most horrible of phenomena.

It was in this world of the abyss that Lucas was dwelling, and to whose influences he was exposing the only being he had ever cared for. He knew, both from the teaching of the occult school in which he had been trained and by his own experiences since he had quitted the physical body, what cold hell of disintegration it was to which he had come. He also knew that, should he fail to keep his footing in the world of manifestation – should he no longer be able, through depletion of vitality, to hold his tenuous form together, then he would be drawn again into the flow of the cosmic laws, and the process of death, which by his knowledge he had been able to hold in abeyance, would continue its course. The last shred of etheric substance which served to anchor him to the world of matter would fall away, and his naked soul would depart to the place of judgement to face its reckoning. For there was a balancing of accounts at the end of each incarnation. Then, the balance having been adjusted by subjective realization, the soul was ready to embark upon a new venture in the world of matter. Experience having been transmuted into faculty and a balance struck between the good and evil of its nature; it had, as it were, realized its assets and acknowledged its debts. Lucas was an absconding debtor, he dared not present himself for examination because his transactions in the unseen powers had been fraudulent. He had employed cosmic powers for personal ends. An account would be demanded of him which he could not give, and he had little mind to face the consequences.

Having no physical organs that could draw energy by the processes of digestion, he had to obtain his energy ready-made from those who had – he thus became a parasite, living upon the vitality of others. Had such mysterious child-deaths taken place in the Middle Ages they would have been recognized for what they were, and a vigorous vampire-hunt set on foot. The body of the suspect would have been dug up, and if it were found to have resisted decomposition it would have been burnt to ashes.

CHAPTER TWELVE

Veronica awoke to find the fire shrouded in grey ash and the dawn-light looking in at the windows. It had frozen hard in the night, and the sun rose upon a silver world. Lucas was gone, but the atmosphere of his presence still hung about the room. The girl flung open the windows and stepped out into the clean coldness of the autumn dawn. Veronica stood, face to the east, waiting for the sun to clear the hills, for though the sky was alight, the valley lay in shadow.

For a while she listened. Cocks crowed on distant farms, and a clop-clop of heavy hoofs on the high-road showed that the plough teams were going to their labours. The still, mist-laden air of the valley began to throb with the sound of human activities. The harsh panting of a loco-motive as it breasted the grade out of Beckering Junction gave rhythm, and Veronica set herself to pace the terrace until such time as her ancient domestic should elect to serve breakfast.

Veronica had much to think about. To her mind had come a lucidity it had never before possessed, and behind the train of memory-pictures she could discern the causes that linked them together. Some door within her conscious-ness had been opened during the night's experiences. In these new regions of the opening subconscious she found a series of memories of herself under different circumstances and these she recognized to be memories of previous lives. She knew that she had formed a tie with Lucas at some time during these lives, and that it was the influence of this tie which she still felt.

As she studied the dream-pictures, they grew clearer. Temple and grove and great resonant rituals built themselves up before her inner vision in elaborate fantasies. These were akin to the scenes she had witnessed when Lucas drove her across the spinning barrier of psychic force that guarded the forbidden degrees of his own Fraternity. These things, if not identical in form, were similar in force, and some connection existed between them.

But these new chambers that had opened in her mind were not only stored with picture-images, but with a forgotten lore that, fragment by fragment as associations touched it, came back into memory. The subconscious was becoming conscious, and in its depths were found stored the memories of her past lives. In the bright dawn of human life, when the unseen world had been very close to mankind and the priest-kings still ruled their peoples, she had entered the mystery-schools that then flourished and had there learnt to work with one with whom, when once the bond was established, she had worked again and again until there came a life of crisis in which one was tempted and fell to the lust of power, while the other held firm to the faith. Veronica, with her widened vision, was now able to read behind the incidents, and knew that the one had been able to enter the great new tide of spiritual life that had been poured out upon the world from the hills of Galilee, whereas the other had sought the old pagan mysteries, had turned from the future to the past, and reverted to a primitive type.

In the present life Veronica knew that they had come together again, but the end of the story was not yet written. Intuition revealed that the one had dealt with the forces of the mind, and the other with the forces of the heart; and that each, deprived of the other, was baffled. The one was a mind without conscience; the other, feelings without understanding. Together they could touch the heights.

Realization had come to Veronica and was dawning in Lucas, but they were in the thick of a toil of consequences that past lives had set swirling about them, and it might well be that realization had come too late for any solution to be found in the present incarnation. Veronica could not see her way through the maze, and she realized that Lucas, in the strange, morbid, life-in-death and death-in-life to which he had condemned himself, might well pass beyond the power of any aid, human or divine, and be drawn into the gulfs of Chaos, whence there is no return.

Smoke rising from the kitchen chimney showed that breakfast was at last under way, and Veronica was turning towards the house when a footstep attracted her attention, and she saw, approaching through the dew-laden shrubberies, a figure voluminously garbed in an old-fashioned Inverness cape and laden with an antique Gladstone bag, and in another minute her old friend of the long white beard stood before her and grasped her hand in greeting.

Amazed beyond words at this unexpected visitation, Veronica entirely forgot the duties of hospitality, and it was not until the old man had led her into the billiard room and divested himself of his wrappings that she inquired the reason for his journey.

He shot a keen glance at her from under his heavy grey brows.

'Did you not expect any one?' he said.

Veronica looked at him blankly for a moment, and then, remembering the promised visitor of her vision-dreams, hesitated, uncertain whether to speak or not, for, though she herself was fast becoming more certain of the reality of her experiences and had ceased to attribute them to imagination, it had never occurred to her that anyone else might share them, and she feared to expose herself to ridicule or suspicion should she reveal her knowledge.

'Yes,' she said slowly, 'I was expecting someone, but I was not quite certain – I did not know it would be you – it took me by surprise when I saw you.'

The old eyes, strangely brilliant in that faded face, continued to study her acutely.

'Who was it told you to expect someone?' he asked blandly.

Veronica returned his gaze squarely, she knew that she was being tested. The old man's thoughts were perceptible to her, and she felt that hers were equally so to him; concealment between them was both useless and needless. 'They told me,' she said simply.

'Then you know them?'

She bowed her head. It was sufficient. They understood each other.

The old woman appeared with a laden tray, and seeing a second person present, shuffled off to boil another egg. Nothing ever perturbed her or seemed to rouse her curiosity. Had she found the Cham of Tartary confabulating with Veronica, she would have boiled him an egg without question. Lucas had trained her well.

The meal was occupied with the courtesies of the table and inquiries as to Veronica's health and other mundane matters. Both felt that there were things to be told that were too momentous to bear the interruptions necessitated by eating, but as soon as the old man was ensconced in one of the big leather armchairs, and his pipe was well alight, he looked across the fireplace to where Veronica occupied the other armchair, and remarked: 'Things, I take it, have been happening?'

He invited confidences, and Veronica determined to burn her boats behind her and give them.

'Dr Latimer,' she said, 'I am going to tell you the truth; perhaps you will think I am mad, but it *is* the truth, whether you believe it or not.'

'I expect I shall believe it,' the old man replied.

'After you left me,' Veronica began, 'everything was quiet for a little while, and I began to think that I had made a mistake and that death was – what most people think it is. But, on the other hand, I felt it wasn't, and that presently

139

I should be wanted.'

'You neither heard nor saw anything?' questioned the old man.

'Nothing. I simply had a kind of feeling, but it was so vague, and so faint, that I could not make out anything definite. One day I happened to put on an old coat that had belonged to Mr Lucas, and that seemed to put me right back into his atmosphere again, and I knew that he wanted me to go down to his grave. I had never been, because I did not wish to think of him as dead, but when I got that feeling I obeyed it and went.' Veronica glanced furtively over her shoulder. 'When I went to the graveyard,' she said, 'I saw four children's graves, all newly made, and this is a tiny village, only one street.' She paused and looked sharply at the old man to see what he would make of this statement. He nodded.

'I am not surprised,' he said.

'There have been other children who have died since then: two others that I know of. I will tell you about them presently, but I want to tell you about Alec first. I got to know him when I went to the churchyard. He was very kind and showed me where the grave was. It would have been rather trying, all alone.'

'Did they bury Justin in consecrated ground?' asked the old man.

'I think so,' said Veronica, 'but not in the old part of the churchyard round the church, but in the new part, over against the river, and right up in the far corner of that.'

'That accounts for a good deal,' said the old man. 'A modern Anglican consecration is nothing approaching as powerful as one that was done before the Reformation. They would have spared themselves a good deal if they had allowed Justin to lie in the shadow of the church. Christian charity can rarely be dispensed with safely.'

'Alec walked home with me through the wood. I was rather upset by the visit to the grave, and also I think that he was attracted towards me; after that, he often came to see me, and in the end he asked me to marry him. I think that that was what did it.'

'Did what?'

'Led to his death,' said Veronica, steadying her voice with an effort. 'We had a dog here, and one night it had a queer kind of seizure and –' She hesitated. How could she possibly recount these wild imaginings? 'And it went mad and broke loose and killed Mr Butler,' she tailed off lamely.

'What was done with the dog?' demanded her interlocutor.

'They had it shot.'

'And its body?'

'They thought it had hydrophobia, so they sent its body to the destructor at Ambridge.'

'Good,' said the old man, with an air of satisfaction. 'That is the only thing to do in a case like this. And after the dog was destroyed, did you have any more trouble?'

'Yes, said Veronica, slowly. 'Mr Lucas came here into this very room, and materialized over there where you are sitting.'

'Did anyone see him beside yourself?'

'Not on that occasion, but when they shot the dog a whole lot of people saw him, and the district is simply scared to death, and the old caretaker started drinking and has been drinking ever since.'

'How did he perform the materialization?'

'He had got a certain amount of substance from the children he had killed, and he borrows the rest from me.'

'Borrows?'

'Yes, he borrows enough to be able to materialize and talk to me, and then returns it and dematerializes when he has finished.'

'Has he done this often?'

'Four or five times.'

'What effect does it have on you?'

Veronica hesitated. 'It does not affect me much at the time,' she said at length. 'In fact, each time he does it it

141

affects me less, but I find that I am beginning to want to – to do the same sort of thing to other people. When I went down the lane the other day a little child ran out to me, and I picked it up and cuddled it; it seemed to me as if I could feel the vitality radiating from it. The mother ran out and snatched it from me, and I was thankful, for I realized that I was doing just the same thing as Mr Lucas had done.'

The old man pulled at his extinguished pipe for some time before replying. Finally he spoke.

'Would it be possible to open Lucas's grave without being observed, or should we be obliged to get a permit from the Home Office?'

'I should think it would be quite possible,' replied Veronica. 'But I should not like anything to be done that could hurt Mr Lucas.'

The old man looked at her keenly.

'What is the position between you and Lucas?' he asked.

'There is an old bond,' answered the girl.

'I thought as much. And what may be the nature of that bond?'

'We worked together in some of the old temples, and then, later, there was trouble and we drifted apart. But we needed each other. In fact, I think a great deal of the trouble came from our being apart. He acted as a brain to me, and I was a heart to him. Then in this life we met again, but things were in such a tangle that we can't get them straightened out. Mr Lucas did all sorts of wrong things with me. He doesn't care what he does. And even now he isn't properly dead, and he daren't die completely, and the only way he can keep alive is by taking other people's vitality.'

'Have you ever heard of vampires?' said the old man.

'Yes,' answered Veronica. 'And – and I have also heard of were-wolves.'

Silence fell between them.

Finally the girl spoke. 'Do you know what the Second Death means?' she asked.

'It means the disintegration of the personality, the unit of incarnation – and its absorbtion by the individuality – the unit of evolution. The personality is as mortal as the body, it is only the spirit which is eternal. The first death is that of the physical form, and the second death that of the body of desire ensouled by the concrete mind. When that is gone, the abstract mind, ensouled by the divine spirit, abides in its own place until the time comes for its reincarnation.'

'Why is Mr Lucas so afraid of the Second Death?'

'Because that is the day of reckoning whereon the personality has to answer for its doings. Lucas dreads the day of reckoning, and not without reason, either.'

Lucas never appeared during the hours of daylight, it was only as the darkness came on that he might be expected, so Veronica showed the old man over her little estate, and pointed out the different objects that were connected with the problem they had to solve. They had visited Lucas's bedroom, where the last blooms of the red rambler shed mildewed leaves upon the windowsill. As the old man gathered them thoughtfully into his hand, Veronica felt that he was surveying the scene with other senses than his five physical ones.

They inspected the empty dog-kennel, beside which still lay the unbuckled collar attached to its chain, and then, from a discreet distance, they surveyed the cottages in the lane. Finally they followed the wood path that led to the churchyard and stood beside a mound of rough earth that was slowly subsiding under the autumn rains.

For a long time the old man remained bare-headed beside the mound, musing upon who knows what. Finally he knelt and laid upon the wet earth the handful of rain-beaten blooms that he had gathered from the rambler that encircled the dead man's bed-chamber. Veronica also knelt, and shaped the dull red flowers into the semblance of a cross.

143

The evening saw them gathered in the familiar billiard room. The wood fire threw its uncertain light, and as soon as the old woman had removed the evening meal, Dr Latimer extinguished the lamp.

'In the ordinary way,' said the old man, 'I should not allow you to go into trance without taking the proper precautions, but under the present circumstances we must leave the gates open and allow what will to come through, otherwise we might exclude something which was essential.'

They had not long to wait. As the flames died down and the logs sank to a red glow, Veronica felt the draining of her substance which showed that her resources were being drawn upon, and once again the cowled figure began to form itself in the shadows. The mist-like exudation condensed itself into floating draperies in the folds whereof hands and features slowly appeared, with pools of illimitable blackness for the eyes.

His attention being concentrated upon Veronica, it was not until fully materialized that Lucas perceived the presence of a third person. Instantly his form shot up to twice its normal height, and the draperies spread out into great bat-like wings as he hovered over the venerable white-bearded figure sitting motionless in the depths of the chair. So readily did the tenuous ectoplasm respond to the ensouling mind that great claws sprang out at the ends of the fingers as they stretched towards the throat of their intended victim. There they hovered for a moment, irresolute. But the clear brilliance of the blue eyes never wavered under their heavy white eyebrows, and the threatening, overhanging form slowly retreated, the spreading bat-wings were indrawn, till at last, in the exact semblance of an Egyptian mummy, Lucas stood upon the defensive.

At length the old man spoke.

'Greeting, my son, in the name of Those whom we both serve.'

A quiver ran through the rigid form confronting him, and

144

a thin fold of drapery seemed to shake itself free from the swathing mummy-bands and hang like a long, loose sleeve.

'Whence come you?' came the questioning voice, as if in some set formula of ritual resonance.

'From the Abyss,' came at length the unwilling answer.

'And whither go you?'

There was a pause, broken only by the slow ash falling in the fire and the rhythmic breathing of Veronica. The log had burnt through and broken before the answer came, but the old man never stirred.

Then Lucas spoke.

'I am in Outer Darkness,' he said. 'Blown about by the winds of space. It is useless to ask me whither I am going, for I cannot tell you.'

'Depart, my son, depart, and be at peace,' said the old man. 'Face your reckoning and meet it, and then, when the day of life dawns for you once more, you can return to the Path whence you have turned aside.'

The bat-like wings unfolded themselves threateningly from the drapery as Lucas answered angrily, 'It is not in your power to bid me depart. I have made good my foothold on the plane of manifestation. We can defy you, between us.'

The old man turned to Veronica. 'My daughter,' he said, 'it is not in my power to make Justin face his reckoning, as he very truly says, because I cannot drive him out of the form he has built for himself without shattering you, for it is built in part of your substance, but if you will withdraw yourself from him, then I can send him to his own place.'

Veronica slowly raised herself up in her chair and looked from one to another of the two who confronted her. To her psychic condition, neither of them seemed material, but to be different types of force, each expressed through the vehicle of a mind. The old man appeared to her as a prism, transmitting a ray from a great sun hung in space, but Lucas shone with a phosphorescence, luminous as certain fungi are luminous, with the light of their own putrefaction.

'Where will he go?' she said at length. 'Where is his own place. Will it be well with him there?'

Lucas laughed, and the sound seemed to be taken up by innumerable voices. Every flicker of firelight, every draught of the crazy house seemed to cackle with ghastly merriment.

'My own place,' he said, 'is the Dark Planet of Disintegration, the Wandering Planet, that has no orbit. There I shall be returned, cell by cell, molecule by molecule, atom by atom, to the primordial substance whence I arose, for it will not be Purgatory I go to, but annihilation, for I have given myself unreservedly to darkness.'

'Are you quite sure, my son, that you have given yourself unreservedly to evil?' said the old man.

'It is not my fault if I haven't!' snarled Lucas.

Veronica's voice cut across their dispute. 'I could not send him to destruction, Dr Latimer. I may be very foolish and very wrong, but I really could not do it. I do not think he can do anyone any harm if I won't help him, and perhaps if we give him time, he may have a chance to put things right.'

'Time is the one thing we cannot give him, my dear. There is no slack water in the cosmic tides. He must go one way or the other, back into life or out to the death of the soul.'

'Then why can he not come back, if such a thing is possible?'

'Because he can only come back through you, and then you will be where he is now.'

'Is that so very terrible?' said Veronica.

'It is,' said Lucas, briefly.

'For the second time,' said the old man, concentrating his gaze upon the shrouded figure before him. 'Where are you going, my son?'

Lucas did not answer.

'Do you intend to go to your reckoning?'

The bat-wings folded closer round the swathed figure

146

and a shudder seemed to run through it.

'Not if I can help it.'

'Then do you propose to maintain yourself in manifestation by means of the life-forces of this girl?'

There was a long pause as Lucas seemed to be unable to come to a decision.

'It will have to be one or the other,' said the old man.

'I know that,' said Lucas.

He looked at Veronica as she lay back in the big chair, and she leant towards him anxiously.

'I do not know what it all means,' she said, 'but I shall not send you away, I said I would stand by you and I will. I cannot let you hurt the children, but I will not send you away myself.'

Lucas smiled a crooked smile.

'I may have to send myself away.'

The old man became tensely still in his chair, and seemed hardly to breathe as he waited for the next words from the grey shadow in the corner.

The fire had died to darkness before they were spoken.

'There are some things –' the words came slow and heavy, like drops of water falling in a cavern, '– which cannot be done.'

Again silence fell upon the room, unbroken by any sound, within or without, and finally the voice of Lucas spoke again.

'If it were anyone but you, Veronica – no, it cannot be done.' Then the voice, gathering strength, rang like a bell, and into it came a note that was almost joy. 'This is good-bye, Veronica. Good-bye and God bless you, go free and be happy. Forget as much as you can and forgive the rest. Or, if you must remember, then remember that I loved you.'

Veronica rose up in the darkness and faced him, and the old man, watching, saw that the child Veronica was no more, for the soul which had lived through the ages had at last entered into full possession of its tenement.

'I shall forget nothing, and there is nothing to forgive.

147

This thing had to be, and we have worked it out together. If you go to the Dark Planet, I will go with you, and if I remain here, you will return to me.'

'It is not for us to say what we will do,' said Lucas. 'I go to Those who will deal with me as They see fit –' and throwing up his hand he cried in a voice of evocation '– for I go to my reckoning.'

The utterance of the words seemed to bring with them a sudden change. The cowled grey figure was shot through as with streaks of fire, and crimson fumes rolled up all around like the light of a burning city. Once again the cackling laughter rose up from every shadow and crevice of that haunted house, and peal upon peal of hooting merriment answered from high overhead where the night clouds raced across the face of the moon. It seemed as if every patch of gloom harboured triumphant evil and Lucas had been delivered into its hands. A blast of furious gale struck the house broadside till the place rocked on its foundations, rafters and beams creaking as if the whole crazy structure were coming down. The windows, torn bodily from their frames, crashed on to the floor in a shower of flying glass. Something that was thicker than the darkness swept into the room with the gale, passed swiftly over all its surfaces, touching them with intangible tentacles till it found that which it sought, and then swept out again as it had come. The gale sank as suddenly as it had arisen; the room, vacated of all presences, was simply a shattered human dwelling-place wrecked by a cyclone. No trace remained of the forces that had swept it or the passions that had invoked them, save only that an intolerable stench of putrefaction rolled up in waves from the corner where the grey cowled figure had stood.

CHAPTER THIRTEEN

The terrific wind died away as suddenly as it had arisen, leaving the room in utter darkness. Veronica could hear the old man fumbling for the matches. The little pale flame lit up at last, a feeble gleam among the shadows. The lamp, smashed to fragments, lay in a corner, and the old doctor turned slowly round, seeking for something to light. As he turned, he suddenly stopped with a half-strangled exclamation, for, framed in the shattered window-space, stood the figure of a man. They both gazed at it in speechless amazement as the dying flame of the match illlumined the strange, impassive countenance, exaggerating with its flickering shadows the deep lines of the parchment skin, the hollow cheeks, the high cheek-bones, the great jaw, and the lofty forehead. The eyes, deep-set and glittering, were those of the hawk. He gave the impression of tremendous power, utterly impersonal, completely under control. Veronica had seen enough of the members of the mysterious Fraternity in whose headquarters she had been concealed to recognize the sign manual of its discipline. The glittering eyes of Dr Latimer, the catlike movement of Lucas, the sense of impersonal power of the hard-faced man, all these she saw developed to a far greater degree and concentrated in a single individual. She knew without telling that this man had to do with the Fraternity, but was far higher, far bigger, than the men she had so far encountered in the handling of its affairs. He as far transcended Lucas as Lucas transcended herself, and she knew without telling that he was not only a man to be obeyed, but to be trusted.

The match burnt itself out in the old man's fingers while he gazed speechless at this apparition, and the room was once again in darkness and silence.

The voice of the stranger broke the spell.

'You know me?'

'Yes, you are – you are – the Third,' said Dr Latimer.

'Quite right. I am the Third. Now I suggest that you strike a light. There are matters I wish to discuss with you.'

Veronica could hear the footsteps of the stranger as he crossed the bare parquet. He moved in the darkness with the precision of a man who could see where he was going, and the clink of metal told her that he had laid his hands on the two brass bedroom candlesticks that stood on the table near the door. By the time Dr Latimer had got the match alight, he was standing before him, holding the candlesticks.

Veronica could now examine him at her leisure. The loose frieze overcoat he wore exaggerated his height and the massiveness of his frame, but as he laid it aside she saw that he was clad in the ordinary lounge suit of civilization. Unlike some students of the occult, the members of this fraternity, which really possessed power and knowledge, did not seek to be impressive, but rather to conceal themselves under the bushel of convention in order to pursue their studies undisturbed.

He knelt before the smouldering hearth and drew the ashes together gently, as if handling living creatures. The instantaneous blazing of the fire under his hand seemed to Veronica of a piece with his power to move in the darkness. He might wear ordinary clothes, but he was no ordinary man.

For the first time he looked directly at her as she sat motionless in her big chair, as she had sat ever since his entrance.

'Come, my child,' he said, laying his hand on hers. 'Draw up to the fire and warm yourself. You are cold.'

150

That kindly touch, which had nothing of a man's familiarity in it, told Veronica yet more about the stranger. Dr Latimer had brains and kindness, but no strength. The hard-faced man had brains and strength, but no kindness, and even as she thought of her old opponent, a step sounded on the gravel of the terrace, and his burly figure stood framed in the window.

He looked just as surprised to see the man who had called himself the Third as Dr Latimer had looked, and Veronica had a secret suspicion that he was not any too pleased. He was not the type of man who would take kindly to yielding, and the stranger would certainly rule any group in which he found himself. On the other hand, she knew intuitively that Dr Latimer was immensely relieved at the intervention of the unknown man, and quite ready to trust the issue into his hands.

'If you will be good enough to come in, Mr Fordice,' said that personage, 'we will be able to close the window.'

The hard-faced man gave a grunt that sounded rather resentful of even this reasonable request, but nevertheless he did as he was asked, and lent his assistance to secure the mouldering shutters that threatened to fall bodily into the room.

No questions were asked or answered, but nevertheless, Veronica, with her quickened intuition, felt certain that each of these three men had obeyed a silent summons, though whether that summons had issued from the Third, or whether he, too, had been summoned, she could not tell. They were gathered in a semi-circle round the now blazing fire, and two pipes and a cigar were rapidly obscuring the atmosphere, and still no word was spoken. She felt that these men were 'sensing' the state of affairs, 'sensing' each other, and acting and reacting in a way which she could not divine. She had always thought that occultists were ascetic people who touched neither meat, drink, nor tobacco, but Dr Latimer had always eaten without a murmur whatever the caretaker had chosen to set before him, and the Third

151

was smoking a long black cigar that would have put the average man upon his back. They might be psychics, but they were certainly not sensitives.

Finally the Third spoke. 'We must settle this matter as speedily as possible,' he said. 'Time is an important factor in the case.'

'I thought it had been settled,' said the hard-faced man, with something that closely approached a sneer.

'I thought so, too,' said Dr Latimer, looking up in surprise. 'Lucas, in my hearing, accepted his fate and went out to the Judgement Hall of Osiris.'

'And was turned back at the gate,' said the Third, 'for his time was not yet come. They would no more accept him than they would accept a murdered man or' – he paused significantly – 'a suicide.'

'Would you consider,' said the hard-faced man, 'that a criminal who was executed in accordance with the law was a murdered man?'

'The law of the land rules the land,' said the Third, 'and when the Race Spirit takes a life, it is a death according to the law, and therefore a natural death. Whether it is right or wise to take that life, is another matter, and in any case the issue is one we are not concerned with here, for the law was not invoked. It was a private vendetta, gentlemen, and it is no use pretending otherwise, and the consequences of your rash action you must face, for you have caused a soul to leave its body before its natural term had arrived, and that soul, therefore, "walks" as surely as any other suicide.'

'Why do you keep on emphasizing the word suicide?' asked the man he had called Fordice, peering sharply at the Third.

'Because I do not know what other word to use for a man who voluntarily vacates his body, the makers of dictionaries had not foreseen such an eventuality as the one we are discussing. No, gentlemen, with all your cleverness you did not even succeed in "bagging" our friend. He eluded you.'

Fordice gave a sound that was almost a snarl. He was

152

evidently more annoyed to learn that his magic had failed of its purpose than relieved to find that he had not got a crime on his conscience. His character appeared to have undergone a profound change even during the short time that Veronica had known him; the evil of which Lucas had rid his soul seemed to have entered into him.

'The question is, what do you propose to do with our friend?' continued the Third. 'He is a member of your Lodge, gentlemen, it is your problem.'

'The reason he does not go to his last account is that he is a vampire,' said Fordice. 'If you opened the grave you would probably find his body as fresh as when it was buried.'

'Precisely,' said the Third. 'We all know that. But the question is: What are you going to do about it?'

'You also know the traditional way of dealing with vampires, no doubt?' answered his opponent, the sneer appearing openly on the surface of his expression.

'I knew it before you were born,' said the Third, a slow smile stirring the lines of his face. 'But, considering the circumstances under which this man became a vampire, would you be justified in using it. You, of all men?'

At this home thrust the hard-faced man winced and kept silence.

'It has always been my belief,' said Dr Latimer, 'that Justin, with all his faults, did not enter our Fraternity without a reason, and it is also my belief that when he gave himself as a voluntary sacrifice to save another, he wiped out a very great deal, if not all, of his debt.'

'Did he not contract a fresh debt when he elected to become a vampire?' asked Fordice.

'Admittedly. But do you not think that he wiped that out also when he went voluntarily to the Second Death? Remember, we had no power to force him to surrender his wraith-form, he laid it down of his own free will rather than injure one whom he loved. The Second Death is a terrible thing for a man in his position to face, and he had no

153

means of knowing that the Second Death would reject him.'

'And even if he had known it,' interposed the Third, 'to wander homeless in the Intermediate State is a much worse thing than to burn in Hell, for you suffer all the pains of purgatory with none of its purification. That soul is out on the astral now, where, between you, you have dispatched him.

'Now, gentlemen, as I told you before, time is the essence of the contract, for, deprived of his peculiar form of sustenance, Lucas will no longer be able to hold his physical body together, and you have just about the same time in which to act as would elapse between death and burial in the ordinary way. Lucas has returned to his grave by now, for it is past cock-crow, and he will probably return to it again tomorrow, but I doubt if he will be able to use it much longer.'

'The correct thing to do is to "Bury him at four cross roads, with a stake in his inside," ' said the hard-faced man, his sneer again getting the better of his discretion.

His interlocutor looked at him sharply. 'Don't talk nonsense,' he said. 'That is nothing to do with the matter. The body will disintegrate, anyway. Lucas has already renounced his vampiricism. What we have to decide is, whether we will let events take their natural course and leave Lucas to wander as an earth-bound spirit till his time is up, or try to get him back into his physical body, which is at present lying in deep trance in the graveyard.'

The old man sat up with a start. 'Then – then he is not dead?' he said.

'By no manner of means,' said the Third. 'He has performed a very advanced yogi operation. If you were to examine his body, you would probably find that even the injuries inflicted by the post-mortem had been reconstructed. He had been out of his body some time when the death-stroke fell upon it, and had evidently planned to lie in trance until he could arrange to get his body exhumed under the proper conditions, living as a vampire mean-

154

while. Lucas took a very long chance, it was a thousand to one against his experiment succeeding, but as he had managed in holding his form together so long there is a possibility that he might have succeeded had he continued. He is a brave man, and whatever the cruelties by which he had kept himself going, I can forgive a great deal to bravery.'

He paused and looked round the room, studying the effect his words had had upon his hearers. Dr Latimer was gazing at him in eager perplexity. There could be no doubt as to the way his wishes went, but he feared to allow himself to hope too much lest the disappointmnet should be too keen. Lucas had meant a great deal to him, had been like a son to his lonely old age, and he had painstakingly transmitted to him all his laboriously acquired occult knowledge, hoping to see the younger man accomplish the Great Work that had been denied to himself.

The hard-faced man had lost the immobile calm of the trained occultist and had his hand at his moustache, tugging at it nervously. It was obvious that a vindictive temper was striving for the upper hand. He hated having his judgements reversed, he resented the tacit assumption of superiority by the stranger, but he appeared to consider resistance as futile and showed signs of making good his retreat as best he could. He rose to his feet.

'I have given you my opinion,' he said, 'but I don't resist your authority. The responsibility is yours. All I ask is, that you will exuse me from sharing the consequences.'

'That is an absolution I have no power to give,' replied the Third. 'You will not see the end of the consequences of this affair for many a long life to come. But we hold no man against his will. If it is your wish to withdraw, you have my permission to do so.'

The hard-faced man pulled on a heavy leather motoring-coat, his eyes wandering from one to another of the faces before him. For Veronica they held something that almost approached pity: to old Dr Latimer he gave a glance of resentment and contempt: the eyes of the Third he was unable to meet. Nevertheless, he addressed him.

'Things may turn out as you expect,' he said, 'or they may not. Lucas may have succeeded in eluding the Dark Ray or – he may not. But in any case I wish him joy of the leavings of the post-mortem.' With which parting shot he closed the door behind him, and they heard his footsteps die away through the empty, echoing house.

'That, of course,' said the Third, 'is the crux of the matter. What has the post-mortem left? We cannot tell that till we open the grave. Our immediate practical problem is, how to get the grave open. There is one person, however, who has got to be consulted before we commence this undertaking. Now, Miss Mainwaring, what is your feeling about the matter? Do you wish to stand clear of it, also?'

Veronica gazed at him, unable to reply for a moment. The thought of meeting Lucas quickened her pulses and brought a faint flush to her cheeks, but the fear of what such a meeting might mean closed like a cold hand about her heart. The dark hawk's eyes of the strange man before her watched her compassionately, but he made no attempt to help her. It was her deepest instincts that had to give the answer, and no influence must be used to sway the surface.

But Veronica's answer was a foregone conclusion. She had gone too far down this path to turn back, and the Karma of a million years was behind her.

'I will stand by – Justin,' she said, using the Christian name of her sinister lover for the first time. 'For I think he will need me when he comes back.'

'I think so, too,' said the Third. 'In fact, it would have served little purpose to bring him back without you, but the decision had to be free. Pity and duty are no substitutes for love.' He looked at the watch on his wrist. 'It has just gone three; the sun rises at seven-thirty; we have, therefore, about three hours between now and second cock-crow to do that which we have to do.'

'How are we to get the grave opened?' inquired Dr Latimer. 'We have no time to get an order from the Home Office, and clandestine digging is impractical.'

'There are more ways of opening a grave than with a spade,' said the mysterious man with the hawk-like eyes. 'Have you got your robes with you?'

'Of course,' said the old man, and taking one of the bedroom candles departed into the draughty darkness of the whispering, creaking house.

The solitary remaining candle did no more than make the darkness palpable in the big room with its shadowy furniture. The man who called himself the Third sat for a while gazing silently into the dying fire, the dull red glow from its embers throwing strange lights and shadows on his rugged features, making him look like a grotesque idol carved by some forgotten race. He seemed far away in the depths of thought, oblivious of his remaining companion, and Veronica was able to study him at her leisure, wondering what manner of discipline had made him the man he was. Suddenly he looked up, and crossing the hearthrug, sat down on a chair close beside hers, taking her hand in his.

'My child,' he said. 'Do you realize what lies before you? Have you any understanding of the matter?'

Veronica gave him her slow Mona Lisa smile. 'I understand better than you think,' she said, 'I have known these things before.'

'And you remember? Yes, I see you do. That is good, very good. I believe we shall be able to carry this thing through with your assistance. To rouse Lucas from his trance is a simple enough matter, but to make him live afterwards, ah, that is the problem. You will have to marry him, my child, do you realize that? And the mating of an occultist is much more than the ordinary marrying. You will have to mate with him in the Unseen as well as on the earth, and in the Unseen, you must be the male force, you

157

must be the controller. Your spiritual nature has got to marry his intellect, and you must fertilize it, not be fertilized by it. Do you understand that? You cannot lean on him on the Inner Planes, by sheer spirituality you have got to take the lead. His mind must never get the upper hand again, your spiritual nature must be the dominant. Child that you are, can you do it? Can you hold a man of that type by his ideals?'

Veronica withdrew her eyes from his and gazed far off into the shadows. Could she do what was required of her? Or had she in her ignorance committed herself to tasks utterly beyond her capacity? No one knew her weaknesses better than Veronica did; she was only too well aware of the simplicity and inexperience that made her a ready prey to the designing, of the diffidence that prevented her from giving effect even to that which she knew, and the lack of self confidence that held her helpless and inarticulate.

Yet within her there was a curious sense of power. Little, bright, clear-cut pictures, like the images seen through the wrong end of a pair of opera glasses, broke and re-formed before her eyes in an ever-shifting kaleidoscope. The portico of a temple, with its great pillars sparkling white in the sun; then the bowed, silent congregation within, the drifting incense and the shifting lights; then the darkness of the Holy of Holies, with the coals in the tripod glowing redly and the dim forms of elemental spirits shaping themselves in the fume.

The man's hands held hers in a grip of iron, his eyes burned themselves into her brain.

'Oh Pythoness!' he said, 'Can you not remember?'

She looked at him with eyes that seemed to gaze through deep water, but as the light cleared, she saw that about his face were forming the folds of the striped head-dress of Egypt; behind him rose the shadow of a vast pylon. His hands crushed hers as his will drove into her, and she could feel the burning heat of them against her skin.

'Oh Priestess of Isis, have you forgotten?' His voice

boomed and rolled like a drum through the room. The shadowy pylon behind him came clear for a moment in rose-red sandstone, then changed into another, though similar, type of masonry, more roughly hewn, though white as milk. Far below her, as if seen from a precipice, the huddled roofs of houses, covered with some yellow metal that was not gold, gleamed dully through the thick, misty air, and the sun hung large in the heavens, like a disk of copper. 'Helios, Helios, Quanto Rhopantanek!' breathed the voice in her ear, and all Lost Atlantis woke to the chant of the Sun-god. She saw the great processions of the white-clad priests and remembered the part she had taken in them: she saw the smoke rise from the sacred volcano, and knew what her function was, and she heard her voice answer in the antiphone, 'Quanto Rhopantanek, Helioun!'

She sprang to her feet and threw up her hands in the Salute of the Sun. The ancient invocation to the Great Initiator sprang to her lips.

'Waft thou my soul down the River of Naradek:
Bring it to Light, and to Life, and to Love.'

The man who was called the Third rose from his chair and gave the answering salute. Through all the changes of the vision, his face had been the one thing that had not changed, under Egyptian nemys or Atlantean filet, it had been the same. He looked deeply into her eyes.

'Do you remember me?' he said.

'Yes,' she answered.

'By what name did you call me last?'

'You were known to us as The Count.'

He nodded, and the tenseness went from his attitude as he relaxed the effort of will he had been making.

At that moment the door opened and Dr Latimer entered, bearing a small black bag in his hand. He laid it on the table beside another of similar shape and size that evidently belonged to the newcomer; then, without instruction,

159

he assisted the man who was called the Third, and also the Count, to shift the furniture into the corners of the room and clear a floor-space. Then he knelt in the middle and held one end of a thread while his companion drew out a circle with a lump of putty-like substance attached to the other end, which left a luminous mark upon the floor, as of some phosphorus compound.

'What sygils?' said he, taking another lump of the same stuff out of his black bag.

'Put the Signs and Seals of the Princes of the Powers of the Air,' replied the other, 'I am going to invoke the Spirits of Tempest. What we cannot dig up we may be able to wash out as the grave is almost on the bank of the river.'

Veronica was reminded of the famous floor-cloth that Lucas had told her about, the thing that first turned his thoughts to the study of occultism. The old man left his companion to compete the hieroglyphs, and put a small piece of some black substance on the glowing embers of the hearth; when it began to smoulder, he took it up with tongs and placed it in a copper thurible of antique workmanship, and sprinkled what looked like fine gravel upon it. A dense cloud of smoke went up instantly, filling the room with aromatic odours and curling into fantastic forms as the draughts took it. He delivered the little censer into the hands of Veronica.

'You must take charge of this,' he said, 'and you must on no account let it go out. Keep it swinging gently all the time.'

They turned to see that the other man had lifted a small table into the centre of the circle and draped it with a black cloth into the semblance of an altar. In a little bowl of ruby glass a floating wick showed a point of flame as it swam on the surface of the sacred oil; its light fell with a ruddy glow on certain metallic objects of peculiar shape that were disposed around it.

Veronica's attention was distracted for a moment by the censer in her charge, from which the smoke had ceased to

160

issue, and mindful of Dr Latimer's warning, she swung it
back and forth till the glowing charcoal once more set the
incense smouldering. She looked up to find that a change
had occurred in the room. The personality of Dr Latimer
had completely disappeared under the flowing black robe
and cowl of an Inquisitor which he had assumed, but the
individuality of the Third was revealed rather than hidden
by his robes, for his cowl was pushed back to frame the
face, and upon his head he wore the royal head-dress of
Egypt.

He came towards Veronica holding out a similar robe to
that which shrouded Dr Latimer.

'This you must wear,' he said, 'for you will need protection in that which we are about to do.'

Veronica, completely enveloped in the flowing black
draperies of the voluminous garment, felt strangely cut-off
from the world. It had evidently been used for rituals before, for its folds were full of the smell of incense.

'Now,' said the Third, 'are we ready? Have we got everything? We can't step outside the circle once we have
started, you know.'

He came towards Veronica.

'This is your place,' he said. 'Whenever you have finished
a circumambulation, come back here, and be sure and keep
the censer going. There is some more incense in that box.
The charcoal ought to last out all right. Always go round
the way of the sun. Be sure you never get into the reverse
circumambulation. Don't try and cut across the circle;
whatever happens, keep going round, and whatever you do,
don't step outside that line. Get the censer going well, and
then walk three times round the circle the way of the sun.'

He returned to the altar, taking his stand with his back to
the East, immediately in front of it. The light from the floating wick threw into strong relief the rugged lines of his face;
and the hawk-like eyes, deep set under heavy brows,
flashed with an unnatural fire. The long black lines of his
draperies added to his height and made him look gigantic

in the shifting shadows, and the golden head-dress of Egypt, with the serpent rising as if to strike from above the brow, seemed the fitting crown for a face that was neither young nor old, but strangely deathless in its calm, as if all the races of the earth had risen and fallen before its un-ageing wisdom and power.

He raised his arms above his head to their full extent, and a great shadow followed him across the ceiling. In his right hand he held a sword, and the towering figure and the flashing blade seemed gigantic among the shadows. The Kabbalistic Cross of purification was marked on brow and breast, and a strange stillness fell upon the room.

At a sign from him, Veronica set out upon her task of pacing the circle. The cowl stifled her, she could see out of the eye-holes with difficulty, the incense rose in clouds into her face as she moved, and at every step she found an in-creased difficulty in balancing. To walk that circle was no simple task, for she seemed to be pushing her way through invisible currents. The second time round, however, was easier, and at the third round a force seemed to push her along, and when she returned to the station assigned to her, she saw that a circle of fire now shone where she had walked. It appeared and disappeared as she gazed at it, and she could not make out what it was that she saw. At first she thought it was an optical illusion, then she thought that something had actually caught fire, and finally she realized that what she saw was not of this earth, and appeared and disappeared as her consciousness wavered between two planes.

The Third dropped the point of his sword upon the symbol on the altar and began the chant of evocation. Vibrant Names of harsh consonants rang out into the dark-ness as demon after demon was reminded of his oath and conjured from the abyss to come to the service of the magus. By the Secret Names of God were they conjured, and by the names of the great Archangels of the Elements;

and as each Name rang out in resonant syllables the atmosphere of the room changed perceptibly.

Demons of storm, Princes of the Powers of the Air, Vice-Regents of the Elements, he called them all by name.

'Oh fiends of the abyss, remember your oath upon the Symbol. Oh dark and mighty ones, remember Who calls upon you.'

The night without was still, pitch dark, and frosty. There was no sound within but the faint shifting of logs on the hearth and the perpetual creaking and whispering of the old house settling upon its timbers. Both men stood like statues, and Veronica, old memories stirring within her, maintained the same stillness, for she had worked ritual magic before, and knew the discipline that teaches immobility.

The evocation ended, dead silence fell upon the room. Force seemed to be pouring in a river of light down the sword on to the symbol, and the figure of the magician was like a dynamo, vibrating with the power of its invisible speed. A faint sigh of wind in the treetops at length broke the stillness; then it came again more strongly, and they heard the scurry of dead leaves over the frosty ground. It was not the kind of night for a thunderstorm, but Veronica was put in mind of the sudden wind that heralds the thunder.

Again the wind rose with a wailing moan, and the snapping of dead twigs in the shrubberies could distinctly be heard above it. And then, without any warning, the crackling volley of thunder broke out immediately overhead, and rain came down in torrents.

Veronica had never seen such rain; it had the violence of a tropical storm, and falling upon the frost-bound ground, it ran straight off down every slope in sheets of water. All about them they could hear the sound of water on the move, and before many minutes had passed, the voice of the river had changed its note.

With the outbreaking of the thunder the tense forces of the

163

room seemed to be released. It was as if the power generated by the invocations had passed from the altar into the cloud, there to be released as lightning and tempest. The two men relaxed their vigilance, and going to the sole remaining window, stood watching the storm.

As the lightning lit up the sky in flickering sheets, they could see the river through the gaps in the trees. It drove before the wind like a miniature sea and had already risen to cover the road. Suddenly a far away roaring, like a train going over a viaduct, fell upon their ears above the din of the storm. It came steadily nearer, as if some heavy vehicle were charging down the cart-track beside the river, and then into their line of vision came a wall of dark water edged with foam that rushed along the surface of the river with the speed of an express train.

'Good heavens, what's that?' exclaimed both men simultaneously. They had evidently bargained for no such manifestation.

In the heaving billows behind the line of foam great timbers rose and fell like the lances of a charging army; part of a hay-rick went past, and then a farm cart, turning over and over.

'A dam must have gone somewhere up stream,' said Dr Latimer, and a big sluice-gate, coming down flat like a raft, confirmed his words. Lucas, terrible in death, was even more terrible in resurrection.

'Quick,' exclaimed the Third, 'we haven't a moment to lose! Heaven knows what that flood-water has done in the graveyard,' and out he went into the raging, buffeting darkness.

Veronica, clutching her censer as if her life depended on it, went after him, the old man, still cowled, close upon her heels.

They made their way through the tormented woods, guided by the squat tower of the church that stood out against the darkness at each lightning-flash. The trees screamed, roared, crashed, and shuddered; branches came

164

down like javelins, and the water ran ankle-deep over the frozen ground that it could not penetrate. It was undoubtedly the frost-bound earth that had caused the catastrophe, for all the water that fell in the valley ran straight down every slope into the river. Thunder-rain usually falls upon parched ground that absorbs a vast quantity before any is thrown off, but frozen ground can absorb nothing, and rain runs off it as off a roof.

They stumbled across the fallen stones of the graveyard wall and found themselves under the lee of the church. The ground rose slightly towards the graveyard, and the road that ran beside the river was cut out of the slope. The swollen river was deep on the road, and raced madly along the retaining wall that held up the face of the bank, and as they approached the spot where Lucas lay, a great spout of foam went up high in the air as a long section of the wall, its foundations undermined, fell into the river.

'Here – here it is!' cried Veronica, stumbling over a low mound of rough earth that lay at the very edge of the water.

'Be careful. Come back,' cried Dr Latimer, seizing her arm. 'More of the bank may go at any minute.'

'It is going now,' said the Third, and even as he spoke, another mass of the bank peeled away, and Veronica had a glimpse of some dark object sticking out of the yellow clay as the moon broke fitfully through the racing clouds. It slowly tilted as the earth was cut from under it by the water, and the loose clods above, washing away in the downpour, revealed the long dark outline of a coffin, which slowly up-ended and slid towards the river.

With one spring the Third was into the washed-out grave and seized the metal handle at the coffin-head that gleamed dully in the moonlight. The bank was crumbling fast, but he stood his ground, and Veronica heard a sound of splintering wood as he forced open the lid of the coffin with some metal tool. The wood was cheap and frail and yielded easily, and as the water reached him, he clambered out of the grave bearing in his powerful arms a long white form, and a flash of lightning revealed to Veronica the features of Lucas, serene in death but unmarred by corruption, swathed in the stained cerements of the desecrated grave.

CHAPTER FOURTEEN

They made their way back through the roaring darkness. The flickering lightning revealed sudden glimpses of the churchyard, with its rows of headstones and black writhing yew-trees rent by the storm. The ground was sodden by now, and the two men slipped and staggered with their burden, leaving Veronica to follow as best she could, still clutching the censer, which for some unknown reason, had managed to remain alight. The girl hoped and prayed that no one would look out from the upper windows of the cottages and see them in the fitful moonlight. What they would make of the black-robed, ghoulish procession, she could not guess, but she knew it would certainly be attributed to the Grange, and even that stolid countryside had reached the point when it was nearly ready for a lynching.

They were still far from the shelter of the wood when her fears were realized. She heard a window thrown up in the neighbouring darkness. Then she heard a door open and shut. So far as she could judge, the sound came down the wind, indeed, it could hardly have been heard from the contrary direction, and she guessed that it came from the house of Dr Butler, whose garden abutted on the churchyard.

'Hurry, hurry,' she cried to her companions. 'Someone is coming.' They struggled on towards the shelter of the wood, guided by the line of tormented yew-trees, and as they passed the gap in the wall, Veronica, gazing over her shoulder in terrified apprehension, saw the flash of an electric torch by the corner of the church. Her companions hurried on, but Veronica paused, she felt that she must see who came and what was discovered. The moon broke through a rift in the clouds, and she distinctly saw a bulky figure clad in the white macintosh that Dr Butler often wore. What strange fatality, what invisible link caused this man invariably to appear when anything was toward with regard to Lucas?

She saw him pause suddenly, as if he had heard something. He looked about him as if trying to identify the direction of the sound. She wondered what it could be. Then he set off and made a straight line towards the place where she was hidden. An eddy of wind from the lee of the woods had carried to him the odour of the incense from the censer she still bore with her. She crouched among the bushes like a hunted creature, petrified, unable to move. The man came on till he was some thirty feet from the edge of the trees, and paused irresolute. The eddying draughts around the yew-trees had carried the tell-tale fragrance away. He was not a primitive savage, and his nose gave him no sure information. She saw him stand there irresolute, and then, believing himself to be alone in the darkness, he lifted his arms above his head and poured out an incoherent mixture of prayer and cursing in which her own name was mingled with that of Lucas and Alec. Then he turned and stumbled off over the grave-mounds in the direction of his home, taking with him his grief and his suspicions to brood over in silence.

Veronica rose from her hiding-place and followed the half-obliterated path through the woods, a sudden realization coming to her that she was alone in the darkness and storm with all the unseen presences of the abyss let loose about her. The storm was not merely a hurricane of wind and rain, it was unspeakably sinister, like hands reaching out from the shadows, and the darkness was palpable, like veil upon veil of soft black woven stuff. But even as she realized the subtle intangible influences abroad in the night, a change began to make itself felt. The howling tumult of the storm was being penetrated by a musical note, which gradually dominated its numberless discordant voices. Slowly they were dominated, gradually they were drawn into tune; then the rhythmical singing itself fell silent and all was still. The storm had died away as suddenly as it had arisen.

All about her Veronica could hear the drip of moisture; little wandering eddies of draught blew in all directions, and the whisper of innumerable streamlets sounded in the darkness. The sudden stillness after the din of the storm left a singing in the ears, the cessation of the lightning gave the eyes a chance to become accustomed to the darkness and use what half-light came from the waning moon. Veronica hastened down the sodden path, going knee-deep into the channels of new-formed streams, pushed through the sodden shrubbery, and mounted the steps from the lawn, just as Dr Latimer stepped out on to the terrace to come in search of her.

A banishing ritual had evidently been done in the billiard room of the old house, for the altar had been dismantled of its symbols and the lamp extinguished.

The body of Lucas lay upon the long sofa beside the fire. The grave clothes had been replaced by one of the black robes worn by the brethren of the Fraternity, the stains of the soil were removed, and the black hair, that had grown long and shaggy, had been roughly cut and smoothed. There was nothing in his appearance to shock her, except that the eyes were deeply sunken, giving an indefinably deathlike look to the face. Otherwise he might have been lying there asleep.

The Third, still in his sodden robes, stood beside the window, evidently awaiting her arrival.

'Go quickly,' he said, 'and change into dry clothes. We have none too long for the resuscitation, it must be completed before cock-crow. Now hurry.'

Veronica needed no second bidding. She fled up to her room and hastily changed her dripping garments and was

169

back again in the billiard room before the fumbling fingers of old Dr Latimer had completed his toilette. The Third still stood beside the inanimate form of Lucas, and as she came timidly up to the couch, he put his arm round her and drew her towards the body of the dead man he had told her she must marry. Together they stood looking down into the masklike face with its sunken eyes.

Veronica was too dazed and numb to know what she felt towards the man who lay before her. The fact that corruption had not touched him convinced her that it would be even as the Third had said, and that Lucas was in a deep trance and capable of resurrection. All thought of his death and burial was obliterated from her mind. She thought of him as an unconscious man who would shortly recover consciousness, and with whose strange and sinister temperament she would once again have to contend. She remembered all he had been to her and all he had done to her, and if it had not been for the arm of the strange master of men, adept, saint, or sorcerer, whatever he might be, that held her so securely, she felt that, like Ahab, she would have turned her face to the wall and yielded up her spirit. But in him she felt an absolute trust, she knew that it was he who would cope with Lucas, though he had to depend upon her as the instrument of his purpose, and she knew that she would not fail him. Whether her love or her horror of Justin were the greater, she could not have said even to herself, but the mysterious adept absolutely dominated her, not because he controlled her, but because he inspired her.

The old man joined them, and the Third bade him sit at the far side of the hearth while he placed Veronica at the foot of the couch so that her face would be the first thing the dead man should see when he opened his eyes. Then, bending over the inanimate body, he made the same passes that a hypnotist makes when he recalls his subject to consciousness.

He had not long to wait. At the third or fourth stroke a shudder ran through the form of Lucas and he tried to move, but subsided again. Life had not yet reanimated the tissues, it was a mere galvanism of the nerves that followed the movements of the magnetizer's hand. The Third placed his open palm upon the chest of the dead man and slowly raised it up and down; after a moment or two the chest followed the movements and breathing was restored. It was soon obvious that the heart had also taken up its beat, for the face was losing its waxen appearance and assuming a more normal tint, though still bleached like the skin of one who has long been in the dark.

The Third turned to Veronica.

'Speak to him,' he said. 'Call him by name. Make him come back.'

Veronica bent over the foot of the couch.

'Justin!' she said softly, 'Justin!'

A quiver passed over the face of the recumbent man. He stirred stiffly, as if with limbs numbed and cramped, and slowly rose to a sitting position; but his face was still that of a sleeper and the eyes remained closed.

She came to the side of the couch and took Lucas's hands in hers. They were cold with the coldness of a serpent, and as she held them the snake-like fingers slowly closed round hers and gripped them. The man who was called the Third came behind Lucas and placed his palms on either side of his head.

'Lucas! Justin Lucas!' he said in deep vibrant tones like the low notes of a 'cello.

The lips of the mask-like face slowly unclosed and a husky murmur came from between them.

'Do you know who I am?' said the voice of the man who bent over him.

A faint nod responded.

The Third let go his hold on Lucas's head, straightened himself, and resting his elbow on the chimney piece, stood waiting for him to regain full consciousness. The expressionless face, like some carven effigy on a tomb, was gradually losing its ghastly pallor as the slow-moving blood

171

began to circulate through the veins. The deathly coldness was passing out of the hands that Veronica held, and it was obvious that moment by moment Lucas was returning to life. He seemed suddenly to become aware of the hands that held his, and shifted his grip on them as if to feel their texture.

'Is that Veronica?' he said.

Veronica could not speak, but her hands quivered in his, and he bent forward and slowly raised first one and then the other to his lips, and then sank back upon the cushions.

For a long time there was silence, Veronica half-kneeling, half-crouching beside the couch and Lucas lying motionless as if dead, but with a difference; something about him had indefinably changed. He was obviously a man who was neither asleep nor dead, but resting; only his face, with its unopened, sunken eyes, still looked deathlike.

Finally he spoke again.

'What has become of – the man who was here when I – first woke?'

'He is still here,' said Veronica.

'Where?'

'Over there, by the fireplace,' replied Veronica.

Lucas slowly turned his head.

'I can't see in this pitch darkness,' he said. 'Can't you strike a light?'

Veronica, nonplussed, did not know what to reply. The soft warm radiance of the lamp fell full on his face and the room was brightly lit. The Third crossed the hearthrug towards them, and taking Lucas's head in his hands again, turned his face full to the light and gently lifted first one and then the other of the eyelids, revealing empty sockets. He and Dr Latimer looked at each other.

'Removed at the post-mortem,' said the Third.

Lucas swung his feet off the couch and sat upright on its edge.

'Is it necessary to be in the dark?' he said. 'Can't anyone strike a light?'

The Third laid a hand on his shoulder.

'There will be no light for you, my son,' he said.

No one spoke. Lucas raised his hands to his face and felt the sockets of his eyes hollow under his touch.

'Is the room lighted?' he said at length.

'Brightly lighted,' said the Third.

Lucas, his face in his hands, sat for a long time silent. At length he spoke.

'I can't complain,' he said. 'It is just.'

'Well done, my son!' exclaimed the Third.

All Veronica's horror of Lucas seemed gone with her knowledge of his blindness, and she knelt beside him, anxiously watching his face.

He turned his head slowly, from habit, as if looking round.

'Are you there, Veronica?' he said.

'Yes,' came her whisper from close beside him, 'I'm here.'

He put out his hand towards her, and she put out hers, but he missed it, and touched her head. His hand rested on it for a moment, and then dropped to her shoulders, encircling them. He opened his lips as if to speak, and then paused, thinking. The realization of his blindness was gradually dawning on him, and he knew that he could no longer carry out the scheme he had planned. True, he had evaded death and returned to life, but it was death-in-life to which he had returned.

A chorus of cocks rang out from the distant farms.

'My curfew,' said Lucas with a smile, and relapsed into silence again.

The Third took his elbow off the mantelpiece, and drawing up one of the big leather armchairs, lowered himself into it.

'The past is past. Let us consider the future. Have you any plans?'

'None,' said Lucas. 'Do with me what you will.'

'But I have many plans, and since you have put yourself into my hands, I will take you at your word. You must take

173

up your work again.'

Lucas did not answer.

The Third continued: 'As you know, I have been out of Europe for a good many years now. Too many, I am afraid. The Fraternity sank to its embers till you, my son, tried to rekindle it.'

Lucas smiled. 'It certainly showed signs of life in places,' he said.

'Yes,' said the Third, 'you were right, it needed a fresh impulse, but you were not able to do it single-handed. Veronica will be your fitting complement for Inner Plane work.'

Lucas threw up his head like a startled horse, then checked himself.

'What has Veronica got to say to that?' he asked in very level tones.

'She gave her consent before we started on this operation.'

Lucas's arm tightened round her.

'Is that so, Veronica?' he whispered.

For answer she crept closer to him, and forgetful of the onlookers, he hid his face in her hair.

After a moment or two he raised it.

'There is one other person I should like to see,' he said. 'A man who was very good to me in the old days. Dr Latimer.'

'I am here, Justin,' said the old man.

Lucas put out his hand and for a long time he sat silent, his arm round Veronica and his hand in the old man's.

When at length he raised his face it had a very different expression. 'What have I done to deserve such a chance?' he said.

'You have realized your mistake and paid for it without murmuring,' replied the man who was known to them as the Third. 'You have turned again and retraced your steps over the burning coals without flinching. You have passed your tests, my son, you are back on the Path, and the gates stand open before you.'

174

THE SEA PRIESTESS
Dion Fortune

The onset of illness had unloosed the bars of Wilfred Maxwell's soul, unlocking the doors to the dark side of his mind, initiating his communion with the moon herself – the fountain-head of what was to follow. For on meeting the enigmatic Miss Le Fay Morgan, he found she bore an uncanny resemblance to the woman of his dreams – the sea priestess from the land far beyond the sunset, who brought her magic to master the sea that was slowly swallowing up the land.

The woman, the vision and the Moon – three parts of the same experience. An experience which was to bind Maxwell inextricably to an ancient sacrificial cult and would demand the ultimate pledge of both body and soul. . . .

'A strong sense of dramatic values and uncanny literary ability.'   *Book Lover*

60p

STAR BOOKS

are available through all good booksellers but, where difficulty is encountered, titles can usually be obtained *by post* from:

Star Book Service,
G.P.O. Box 29,
Douglas,
Isle of Man,
British Isles.

Please send retail price plus 8p per copy.

Customers outside the British Isles should include 10p post/packing per copy.

Book prices are subject to alteration without notice.